SUBJECTS WE LEFT OUT

SUBJECTS WE LEFT OUT

NAOMI WASHER

velizbooks.com

Subjects We Left Out copyright © 2020 by Naomi Washer

All rights reserved. No part of this book may be used or reproduced in any manner whatsoever without written consent from the publisher, except for brief quotations for reviews.

Veliz Books' titles are available through our website and our primary distributor, Small Press Distribution (800) 869.7553.
For personal orders, catalogs, or other information, write to
info@velizbooks.com

For further information write Veliz Books:
P.O. Box 961273, El Paso, TX 79996
velizbooks.com

ISBN: 978-1-949776-08-9

Cover photo "Dissolution de la mémoire 11" by Laurence Briat
Copyright 2020 © Laurence Briat
All rights reserved

Cover design by Silvana Ayala

SUBJECTS WE LEFT OUT

I have traveled in search of distractions;
I have found none;
and I continually think of France.

> Stendhal

I often believe there is something seriously wrong with me.

I feel a twinge in my neck or my torso or my pelvis and decide that I will soon be dying. My sister says that even if I had only one month to live, I'd still become famous through posthumous publication. We laugh, and then we hang up the phone.

But then I lie in bed at night worrying that my family, with all their good intentions, will publish all the terrible writing they find on my computer—pieces I meant to destroy but kept in case I want to salvage something from them. So then I think I must hurry up and delete all those bad files—to make the process easier on my family after my death, and to ensure my utmost posthumous success.

Still, sometimes I worry that one day there really will be something wrong with me, and I will not be able to tell Alex because I am too afraid to speak clearly with him; and because I am too afraid to speak clearly with him, he will not know that I will soon be dying; and because I will soon be dying, it would be a good time for us to try to start speaking clearly.

In seventh grade French class, our teacher broke down the phrase constructions *J'ai faim* and *J'ai besoin*—*I have a hunger* and *I have a need* is what they mean when you translate them word for word into English. I liked possessing intangible things like need. In class, we read poems about tea; milk in the tea and the spoons; love departing; prisoners in chains. Our teacher laughed so we would not feel sad.

There were quizzes on the subjunctive; the past tense; the present. I took the quizzes. I spoke French with a good accent but found I could not keep up with the passage of time. I knew how everything ended, but somehow I remained in the middle instead.

I took a quiz: conjugate the verb in the present tense. I wrote my answers in the subjunctive: not what *I do* but what *I might do*; not what *I think* but what *I might think*; not what *I feel* or *I say* but what *I might feel*, what *I might say*.

I took my paper to the teacher's desk. He looked over my answers. He could not believe I did not understand the present. He looked at me as though I lived on a plateau very far away. He looked at me as though he could not see where I might be.

I looked back at him from my plateau.

What is the present tense? he asked me. I pointed to my doubtful responses; my hesitations; my might-have-beens. What is the present tense? he asked me again.

I was wrong. I hadn't understood.

What is the present tense, Isabelle? What is it?

The book was called, in French, *Langue entre-temps*; in English, *Language in the Meanwhile*.

The author's name was Isabelle. She'd studied at the Sorbonne when my grad school translation professor spent a semester teaching there. My professor thought we'd like each other's work. Isabelle's book—her first—had recently been published by a small press based in Mortemart, a small town in the Nouvelle-Aquitane region of west-central France. I was drawn to the title, and I liked that her name was Isabelle—the name I'd chosen for myself in seventh grade French class, though it wasn't anywhere close to my actual name. Our teacher had allowed us the freedom to choose our own names; our own personas; our own realities.

Through Facebook, I wrote to Isabelle who quickly helped me retain the rights to the English translation. I liked her photographs on Facebook and Instagram, and she liked mine. She posted images of her books; rain on her windowpanes; elaborately carved, painted doorways. We began using the informal *tu* with each other almost instantly and shared stories about our lives in our respective cities—mine in Chicago, near the north branch of the Chicago River; hers in Paris, near the Saint Martin Canal. *Tu devrais venir me voir !* she said one day, and I agreed: I would love to visit you, I said in French.

Her book arrived a couple of weeks after our initial conversation. It was a lovely edition, printed with a thick, coarse white cover and French flaps, the title appearing in a burgundy script. I read it while riding the train from my apartment on the north side to a café downtown where I liked to work. There were nice cafés in my neighborhood too, but I liked having to travel a bit before I settled into translating. It helped me feel as though I were bridging some necessary distance that brought me closer to the meaning of her text. I would send her a photo through the window of the train of the river below the clock tower—an iconic image of my city. She said it helped her feel closer to the meaning of my translation too.

Language in the Meanwhile was a collection of letter-poems addressed to a guy named Alex with whom Isabelle had studied literature some years before. Alex was an American—*comme toi*, she said, like me—and had returned to his home university in the States after one year. It was clear from the intimate tone of the book that much had been shared between them during his time in Paris, but that they'd also maintained a level of distance.

We knew each other intimately, she said in French, but nothing ever happened.

I knew something about that kind of intimacy. I told her as much in our first conversation. It meant something to her; she said it was the primary reason I should be the one to translate her book. *Tu le connais bien*, she said, because I had experienced a similar thing. She had read some of my writing published online and felt that our work occupied a similar world. These are the two most important things, she said in French: that you write well in your own language, and that you understand what I am trying to say.

I understood what she was trying to say. I understood because I had my own Alex. I'll call him Alex here because it's simpler, and because both guys were similar too. My Alex was an Italian who had studied in my graduate program in Chicago for one year before returning to his home university in Florence. Our time with American Alex and Italian Alex had taken place in the very same year. Isabelle and I were floored by the Alex connection.

What is 'floored'? Isabelle had asked me, and agreed when I explained in French.

Isabelle and I were similar too. Let's call me Isabelle too.

The café downtown where I liked to work was near the Harold Washington Library and below the El station where I'd catch the Brown line train home. The café was furnished with those classic blue American schoolroom chairs. It was the only café downtown that stayed open late.

My city was the kind whose downtown empties every day by 6 o'clock, its residents preferring to return to their warm apartments and families. My neighborhood was full of young families. I liked walking after dark in any season through its quiet, tree-lined streets, peering into the orange glow of first-floor windows and coveting their plant-filled alcoves. It was a walk I'd often taken with my Alex when he lived in Chicago, but now I walked alone.

Sometimes I'd send him a photo of our favorite apartment window on Giddings. But Florence was seven hours ahead of Chicago: if I sent him the photo at 9 p.m. my time, he would receive it at 4 a.m. in Florence. He was often asleep at that point, so he would send back a yellow heart emoji five or six hours later, at 9 or 10 a.m. in Florence and 2 or 3 a.m. in Chicago.

But Alex liked the hour of four in the morning. He would sometimes be awake, reading or writing or translating or spiraling in literary theory. Those nights when he was up at four and sent the yellow heart emoji right away, I felt as close or even closer to him as when he'd lived here, near me, in my city.

The café downtown was also the one where I would meet my translation professor about my work or applying for grants and residencies. We got along well, talking loudly and laughing at the table. A waitress once asked if we were sisters. Occasionally she would ask me how Alex was doing in Florence, but I didn't have the strength to say much about him. I would focus my response on the academic—yes, he's still working on that anthology of contemporary American poets; yes, I did send him a poem of mine—but quickly changed the subject.

Langue entre-temps (1)

Je suis désolée de ne pas avoir pu être un feu, un hiver continu ;
j'invoque la pluie, Fernando Pessoa, un lit plein de vie urbaine.
Dis-moi que c'est vraiment ce que je suis : je suis ce que j'aime.
J'invoque la pluie ; Fernando Pessoa ; un lit empli de la distance
dans laquelle je t'ai aimé.

Language in the Meanwhile (1)

I'm sorry I couldn't be a fire, perpetual winter; conjuring rain,
Fernando Pessoa, a bed full of city life. Tell me this is truly what
I am: I am doing what I love. I am conjuring rain, Fernando
Pessoa, a bed full of the distance in which I loved you.

Who would like to describe, my translation professor asked the class, in what ways a translated text is judged as successful, based on last night's reading?

She called on me.

Success is judged by how smoothly it reads in the target language, I explained, as if it hadn't been translated but is itself the original. And when it reflects the original author's style and intention and the essence of the original text.

The professor began to write a few categories on the whiteboard while I spoke: linear syntax; univocal meaning; current usage; linguistic consistency. Very good, she said, turning back around to face the class. Would anyone like to add anything to that?

The goal, Alex said from across the room—the first time I ever heard him speak—is to, how do you say, minimize the disruption of the signifiers.

Say more, the professor prompted as she sat down on her hands on the front of her desk.

I'd assumed, until I heard Alex's voice, that everyone in the classroom was American. I couldn't immediately place his accent and listened closely as he continued to speak.

It is about creating a nuanced relationship, he said, between the signifier and the signified. We have the signifier, which is the sound or the image of something, like a river, and the signified, which is the idea or the concept of the river.

I sat up straighter in my chair and stopped picking at the skin around my fingernails.

And the river means something different to each one of us, Alex went on. To each reader, the signified is personal. It is internal. I could say to you, for example—he gestured to me, as if randomly, but I noticed that he tried to catch my eye—that I need to "wash my language in the river," but that sentence might mean something different to you, because how do I know what the river means to you?

He held my gaze.

Alright, the professor said, bring the metaphor home.

Alex cut his eyes away from me.

A good translation, he said, smoothes out the difficulty that a signifier can create, the way it can take the reader too far from seeing the source and understanding it.

It's an ethical question, I said before I realized I was saying it. The class was becoming a private seminar between Alex, the professor, and me.

Say more, the professor prompted me.

I could tell she had noticed it too; professors always do.

This idea, I went on, of how to preserve the foreign in the original without alienating the reader. You want to preserve the poetry as much as you can. The sounds, rhythms, alliterations—those are often impossible to replicate exactly. But also the cultural beliefs behind the text. It's an ethical and political problem for the translator to solve, as they try to find a way to shed light on the context behind and present in the text, along with its aesthetics.

Levinas, Alex added from across the room. "The ethical act is to recognize and receive the Other as the Other."

Yes, I batted back, and Berman, from last night's reading: « *desir d'ouvrir l'Étranger en tant qu'Étranger à son propre espace de langage.* » "The desire," I repeated in English, "to open the stranger as a stranger to his own language space."

I held his gaze.

Ultimately, the professor chimed back in, what I want you all to consider this week, as you work on your first translations, is on which side you fall of the two methods laid out by Schleiermacher. She had been writing the Schleiermacher quote on the whiteboard during my tennis match with Alex: "Either the translator leaves the author in peace, as much as possible, and moves the reader towards him, or he leaves the reader in peace, as much as possible, and moves the author towards him."

As I rode the train home that night, I wondered what Alex had meant with that sentence, *Wash my language in the river*. It seemed to resonate with me in a way that I did not feel I had the language to describe. I observed my reflection in the window of the train blending with the building lights outside and the ripples in the water down below. A good translation, I thought to myself as my face disappeared into the landscape, achieves transparency.

When the train reached the Western station about thirty minutes later, I exited through the turnstile at the back of the platform—a shortcut through the parking lot to my apartment. As I crossed the street toward my building and glanced at the lights in the square, past the homeless man who stood on the corner every night outside the Potbelly's, trying to sell copies of *Streetwise* magazine, I thought I saw Alex leap up onto the side of the fountain outside the German bar, then jump down on the other side to continue walking down the street and out of the square. But whoever it might be was too far away for me to really see, so I couldn't be sure.

Langue entre-temps (2)

Tu ne t'en rappelleras sans doute pas, mais un jour, en allant chez moi, tu t'es promené parmi des fleurs sauvages dans le parc. Quand tu es enfin arrivé à mon immeuble et que je t'ai fait entrer, tes vêtements étaient couverts de minuscules fleurs, de morceaux d'herbe et de bardanes. Toute la soirée, pendant que nous parlions d'écriture et de traduction, tu as ôté les bardanes de ton pull et tu les as rassemblées en une pile sur le parquet du salon. S'il avait existé une photo de moi couverte de fleurs sauvages et de bardanes épineuses, cela aurait été la meilleure autobiographie que j'aurais pu écrire.

Language in the Meanwhile (2)

You probably won't remember this, but one day on your way to my place, you trampled through some wildflowers in the park. When you finally arrived at my building and I buzzed you in, your clothes were covered in tiny flowers, bits of grasses and burrs. All evening while we sat and talked about writing and translation, you plucked the burrs from your sweater and gathered them in a pile on the living room floor. If a photograph existed of me covered in wildflowers and prickly burrs, it would be the truest autobiography I could ever write.

The downtown café was one I had frequented with Alex too, typically in the evenings following our translation seminar. We'd drink more black coffee than we needed to that late at night while talking over each other about writing, then ride the Brown line back to the north side where we'd circle the tree-lined streets once or twice before parting ways in the square—him to the room he was subletting on Ainslie, me to my apartment on Leland, where I lived alone.

That square was the place where I met Alex for real for the first time. We'd both moved to the neighborhood in August, before the semester began. It was my first year in the program, and his first extended stay in the States. I'd moved from the Hudson Valley, walking away from my first long-term relationship—if three years can be considered long.

It's difficult now for me to choose my favorite season to sit in the square, but it's very good on late summer nights. During the day it's filled with children, but aside from one or two homeless men or a couple of high school kids kissing on the benches beneath the lampposts, it's largely empty at night. Germans had originally settled there several decades before, so it retained a European atmosphere with its cobblestones, specialty shops, and corner café terraces.

Alex and I both said we felt at home there.

In early October, the translation professor asked each person to describe which languages they felt connected to. Many in the class were not fluent in a language other than English, so they spoke of trips to other countries, lifelong curiosities, and generations of ancestors they wanted to better understand. Once we chose the language we would be studying for the semester, each student brought in a poem we would all practice translating. The student would create a trot—a basic, word-for-word translation—and we would transform it into literature in our own way.

It was satisfying, despite the fact—or because of it—that we did not always understand the original language that someone introduced. More often than not, I found I was able to apply a steady blend of research and intuition to achieve a faithful and creative translation. In mid-October, when it was still warm enough to walk at night but growing cooler, the bright colors of summer shifting to pale autumn hues,

Alex brought in Pavese's poem "Agony":

> Girerò per le strade finché non sarò stanca morta
> saprò vivere sola e fissare negli occhi
> ogni volto che passa e restare la stessa.

> I'll wander these streets until I'm dead tired,
> I'll learn how to live by myself, how to meet the eyes
> of each passing face and remain the same woman.

That was the Geoffrey Brock translation. I left the word 'woman' out of mine.

I sat at my café for a long time, thinking about how to render my translation. I watched all the people hurrying past the café windows and up the escalators to the train. I watched them pull their jackets around their bodies and sling their bags to the opposite shoulder, digging for their transit cards in their pockets. I watched as they did not watch me. I wondered who they were going home to, and why they had to hurry. I had no one to go home to, and it felt as though I never needed to rush. I slipped in between the normal spaces of the day, occupying many unseen corners. Sometimes I made accidental eye contact with people and observed the fear in their eyes at having been seen.

I thought about Alex—his silences in class, which were never blank but always full with many layers of attention. A few times, we had caught each other's eye when the professor or another student was speaking. Although we'd never spoken outside of class, it was clear in those moments that we understood what our eyes were trying to say. I was still new to the city and not close with anyone yet. I recognized something in Alex that resonated with me, though I did not know how or why. I thought if I got my Pavese translation right, if he recognized in my translation what I recognized in the silence of his eyes, he might speak to me.

In class the following week, we read our translations of Pavese out loud. The professor asked why I left the woman out of the first stanza. I didn't see her there, I said.

A few days later, I found a copy of Brock's translation of Pavese's *Disaffections* in my campus mailbox with a handwritten note on a slip of paper tucked inside the front of the book:

Ti ho visto in piazza quest'estate, fumavi sotto il lampione.
Abito anch'io in quella zona. Ci passo ogni sera.

I didn't translate the note I found from Alex right away. Not knowing what it meant in English was too intriguing. Not to mention knowing that, no matter what he'd written in the note, it showed me I'd succeeded in capturing his attention through my translation, just as I'd hoped. So I taped the note on the wall above my desk for a few days and waited for it to translate itself for me, to slowly unfold in a constellation of meaning.

I saw you in the square this summer, smoking under the lamppost. I live in that neighborhood too. I go there every night.

It took some time for me to understand these phrases, not knowing Italian, because I noticed that he'd left the subjects out. I did some cursory reconnaissance on Italian syntax and learned that it's possible to leave out the subject pronoun in a way that you could never do in English. The conjugation of the Italian verb allows the listener to understand which subject has been left out. In the first half of Alex's first sentence, the words *Ti ho visto* translate in English to *You have seen*... seemingly the opposite of what he meant, which was *I have seen*. But *ho* in Italian means *have* and implies *I have*, i.e. *ho visto*; *have seen*; *I have seen*. And me—as the Other, the Subject spoken to and addressed—I made my appearance in the beginning: *Ti* was me.

I wasn't the subject that Alex had left out. The subject that Alex left out was Alex.

Ci passo ogni sera, he wrote, which translates to *There pass every night*. But *passo*, like *visto*, carried the first-person implied hiding inside it, making the sentence's true word-for-word English translation *I pass there every night*.

When I finally took the note down from the wall to translate it, I flipped through the book of poems and noticed that Alex had also folded down the corner of one page and underlined three lines from "Creation":

> We aren't so different,
> we both breathe the same faint glimmer of light
> as we casually smoke, beguiling our hunger.

I was confused. Excited, but confused. I didn't remember seeing him there in the square over the summer and couldn't understand how he'd seen me if I hadn't noticed him. If I'd noticed him so immediately in class, why hadn't I seen him in the square a few weeks before, when he and I could even have been the only people there? Could I have been that consumed by useless thoughts about the person in New York I'd walked away from?

I hadn't seen Alex there, but he had been there, and now he was telling me.

But that confused me too. The note was not explicitly an invitation; it was merely telling me something that was apparently true. I go there every night, it said. It did not say, Meet me there tonight. I didn't know much about the language of Italy and wondered if Italian sentences were less direct, more poetic.

The night I finally translated the note from Alex, I went to the square to see if he might be there. It was late, around 10 p.m. It was autumn, it was still warm. I turned the corner and saw him seated there, smoking and looking up between the branches of a tree.

I watched him from a little ways away for a moment. There was nothing to see, but like I've said before, the nothing of silence can mean everything to me.

To get started with a translation, I often flipped through a book at random to land on a passage I liked. I wanted to see how it would sound in English before I translated the book from beginning to end. The passage would be out of context, but I knew I could only identify a connection with the book if a line I chose intuitively emerged in English smooth and lucid.

It felt similar to flipping through a book I'd read many times before and rediscovering a passage I'd underlined or squared off with brackets and stars. These passages, I knew, were not objectively better than the rest but rather emblematic of some struggle I'd been going through. The more times I reread a book, the more passages there were that became underlined as my struggles changed, evolved, intensified, or faded away. I was re-reading myself to continue avoiding the past tense: even when I knew a particular struggle was gone from my life, re-reading it in the pages of another person's book allowed me to see the way that struggle would go on existing without me—never fading in its truth, only waiting for the next reader who needed to witness it.

I did this with Isabelle's book too, flipping through pages on the train until I found a passage I liked and letting the sounds play out in my head until I reached my apartment or the café where I could write it down. It was sometimes better in the early and late stages of a translation to work at home, alone, so I could speak the original language out loud and whisper the first draft of my version. I needed to hear the sound of the original because the sound carries so much contextual meaning; layers that could be lost if I did not capture them. Speaking the original out loud gave it a power in the room, which is why I whispered my translation: I needed to see—I needed to hear—the English version sidle up beside the original like a sister; like an echo; like two people walking side by side down a tree-lined city street who know each other intimately but do not need to speak.

Langue entre-temps (3)

Tu sais ce que tu veux, tu ne veux simplement pas être le premier à le dire. Tout le monde te voit. Tout le monde voit ce que tu fais. Ils savent que tu recherches la chose la plus difficile à imaginer.

Language in the Meanwhile (3)

You know what you want, you just don't want to be the first one to say it. Everyone sees you. Everyone sees what you're doing. They know you're after the hardest thing imaginable.

When I first read the passage on page 3 from Isabelle's book at random on the train, I knew she was speaking to her Alex. But her language demonstrated that the passage could be speaking to anyone: to herself, or even me, or my Alex.

The first time I read the passage, I wanted to send it to my Alex immediately. But he and I were hardly speaking by then, at least as often as we had before.

For a while, after my Alex moved back to Florence, we talked every day no matter the time difference—from when I woke to when I fell asleep, sometimes with my phone still in my hand waiting for his reply. Every thought, every experience, every photo I took on my phone of the darkening sky was for him, filtered into a way of speaking which I only used with him. Sometimes I would place my phone on the opposite side of the room and wait to hear from him. His reply would arrive with the particular chime of the messaging app, and I would direct all my energy toward him—toward the phone—but remain where I was seated for some seconds.

I didn't understand our compulsion toward each other. I questioned it constantly in my mind and sometimes, if I'd drunk enough wine, with my friends. But the one question I refused to consider was whether this constant conversation meant, in the end, nothing at all.

That's what kept me from sending my Alex the passage from Isabelle's book. I'd grown aware enough of the question that even if I chose not to answer it, it helped me hold myself back from making a fool of myself with my Alex, who was not and never had been "my Alex," and was somebody else's by the time I began to translate Isabelle's book.

"You know what you want," her book told me, "you just don't want to be the first one to say it." It was true; I never had. I never said to my Alex what I had wanted to say, just as Isabelle had never said to her Alex what she had wanted to say. None of that mattered now. Or rather, a new meaning for it all had arrived: Isabelle had written it, and I was bringing life to its translation.

Langue entre-temps (4)

Si l'écrivain ne parle pas ici d'envie, ce n'est pas parce que le désir n'est pas présent.

Language in the Meanwhile (4)

If the writer does not speak here of wanting, it is not because desire isn't present.

The night I finally spoke to Alex in the square, we ended up back at my apartment around the corner where I lit a couple of lamps so we could see, but not too brightly.

Why does this look exactly like the place where you would live, he laughed.

Because it is, I said. Because I do.

I boiled water for two cups of green tea while he browsed the bookshelves. He pulled one out by a contemporary American author with whom he was not familiar and asked me to tell him about it. The book was about reading; interruptions; travel; a never-ending search. I began describing it but decided he should experience it for himself.

You can't borrow my copy, I said. My notes are too personal.

He laughed.

I don't know you well enough yet, I said. Get your own.

Several hours later, unable to sleep in the middle of the night, I drafted an email I never sent him about the dangers of reading. In it, I composed the most serious literary threat I knew how to raise: as a reader, was he brave enough to meet continual deferrals of the plot head-on?

Schleiermacher's theory was that a good translation should provide the reader with the same pleasure and delight that a reader would receive from the original text. He said it was like the reader became a lover; that the foreign language (body) would always remain in some way a mystery to him no matter how close or how familiar he became with the source; that he may not ever be able to grasp the whole, but he can still "enjoy the beauty of the foreign work in total peace." In total peace. I had never experienced total peace as a lover, a reader, or a translator. I knew I was approaching at least one or two of these identities in the wrong way, but I couldn't pinpoint which ones. They kind of blended together for me.

In a high school class on Romanticism, we read the Raymond Carver short story "Why Don't You Dance?" I sat across the room from my ex and argued with him throughout the entire discussion about why the boy in the story should have done what the girl in the story had wanted him to do.

My ex, though I didn't want to admit this at the time, was not comparing the story to our relationship when he stated that it made sense for the boy in Carver's story to disagree with the girl, nor when he gave the reasons why. It was more pleasurable for me, when I was that young, to remain resentful and vindictive, clinging to the version of the story I wanted to believe.

Alex and I didn't speak much anymore. Before (before what?), we had spoken during all our high points, our lows, and everywhere in between. We would say we had slipped into an unproductive *crepa fosso*—a crack / ditch—when our creative lives seemed especially grim. Now I only heard news about his life and publications from his Facebook posts, which were written for *tout le monde*—for anyone who happened to see them, not just for me.

Before, he used to phrase ideas and jokes and questions the way he knew I'd like to hear them. It was exhausting for both of us: we challenged each other, 24 hours a day, to perform at the heights of our creative intellect. I can only speak for myself on record, but I loved every minute of it, and I do believe he loved it, in his way, too.

I tried to keep my relationship with Alex quiet from the other friends I was making at school. It seemed easier not to speak about something I could not explain. At its best, the tense, intimate energy conjured by our connection was not unlike the way I felt when tackling a challenging translation: wrestling with knotty wiring at my desk until it unfurled, revealing a long line of possibility. That's what Alex was to me: a possibility.

But a translation never belongs to you, even when you are the one who creates it. It is always larger; always beyond your grasp; always existing not for you but *tout le monde*, all the world, which is to say for everyone who is able to see what you are doing.

The story of me and my Alex was not the kind of story you share on Facebook when you're hurt and in pain—those posts where people ask for all the world to send them "good vibes" so they get what they want. I made a joke about this to Isabelle, who was surprised to hear about this uniquely American social media practice.

And why should one's luck or misfortune be in someone else's hands? she asked. I think, she said, the French are more accustomed to the common feeling of lost love. It is not the world's responsibility, she said, to give you what you want.

Try telling that to any American ever, I replied.

We laughed.

I said it to Alex once, before he left Paris, Isabelle said. There was a problem with his visa, he was frustrated with his professors and his program in New York, he was miserable for the last few days before he left. I think he did not know where he should go or the best place for him to be. He wanted someone to tell him that everything would be alright, but that wasn't me. I told him he was being such an American, that things do not always turn out alright after all, or the way you want them, at least not at the time you want them or in the exact way you think you want. I was talking about him, but I was also talking about myself. He was leaving, it was the last chance I had to hint at what I wanted. I thought I was being so forward, so direct. I thought it would be impossible for him not to understand my meaning.

We were out for a walk by the Canal, she went on. He had to be packing soon. He was quiet for a long time, looking out at the water with his hands in his pockets, as if I wasn't even there. I think he did forget that I was there. After what seemed like a very long silence, I asked if he wanted to keep walking or go to eat somewhere. He looked at me as though he'd never seen me before. He looked at me like he did not know me, or as if he could barely see me, as if I lived on some plateau very far away. I looked back at him from my plateau, inviting him to join me. But he said he had to go. He paused for a moment, as if he knew he should say more; you know how ceremonial Americans can be, they always have to turn a moment into Something More, something large and final, it seems trained in them from childhood. But the moment passed, and Alex didn't speak. He turned and walked away.

Langue entre-temps (5)

Nuit dans les montagnes, la vallée, la ville, et partout le même silence, sans savoir.

Language in the Meanwhile (5)

Night in the mountains, the valley, the city, and everywhere the same silence, not knowing.

The last time I saw my Alex in Chicago, he'd walked away in a manner similar to how American Alex had left Isabelle in Paris. He had been packing, preparing to go back to Florence, when he sent me a picture of a stack of books on his floor.

What the hell to do with all these? he said. Come save me from myself, take them, put me out of my misery.

I walked through the square where we had sat talking together so often that year. I thought again about how strange it was that I'd never seen him that first summer he had seen me; how there would be no more evenings in the square with him; how he had never once said he might visit Chicago again in the future, never once that I should come to Florence to visit him. It reminded me how angry I really was with him, all the time, that he did not give more of himself to me. *Je voulais tout de lui ; je voulais tout*, though I knew it would never be. I kept hoping, with the same stubborn, persistent desire in which I approached my translations—never giving up hope that a satisfying clarity would come to me.

I tried, while gazing at an empty bench in the square, to see us from the outside; how others might have seen us if they stopped to look or glance for a moment at least. Would they think we were one—the fiction I believed in—or separate, the way we really were? Would they see how much *je lui voulais* in a way I always tried to hide, and would they see how little he had wanted me? I wondered what we must have looked like, sitting there with our legs crossed the same way, smoking our cigarettes the same way, in every season. As I watched the empty bench with these images projecting out from my mind, I saw the warm summer heat give way to yellow autumn leaves covering the cobblestones, the leaves buried beneath a layer of snow, the bare branches of the trees beginning to welcome spring.

A car horn sounded somewhere behind me and jolted me from my reverie, propelling me out of the square and down the street toward Alex's apartment.

We hadn't spent much time there that year. It wasn't an unpleasant place to be, but his roommate, Julia, was particular. She was a law student at another university downtown and kept unpredictable hours in the apartment. We never knew when she would be around. Sometimes she'd come home while we were laughing in the kitchen over some Samuel Beckett meme, and it would be clear that she wanted us to leave. She never spoke much. She probably thought there was something going on between Alex and me. Lots of people did, but they were wrong.

Julia opened the door when I buzzed, and Alex called out for me from his room down the hall. He didn't normally speak so loudly in the apartment, so as not to bother Julia. She gestured toward him, seeming a little pissed off, and returned to her room. I figured the packing had become quite stressful. But when I entered the room, I saw that he was being dramatic as usual; exaggerating; turning some small thing into a mountain, for fun. His suitcase was packed, the room was clean and ready for a new subletter, and the stack of books for me had been moved on top of the desk.

Please, he said in mock exasperation, take them away, take them!

I looked through the stack. There were a few slim collections of poetry I knew he hadn't liked, a novel and short story collection from a fiction class we'd both abhorred, a few memoirs by older American writers that made me fall asleep when I'd tried to read them, and a French copy of Barthes' *The Pleasure of the Text*.

How can you get rid of this? I asked, holding up the Barthes.

It will be much better in your hands, he said briskly, now toss those in your bag and help me get this horrible suitcase down the stairs.

Four hours till my flight, he said without looking at me. Those seven thousand dollar airport French fries are calling out to me, come on.

His suitcase on the street; his passport in his pocket; the cab on its way, four minutes around the corner. So you're going, I said with my arms crossed, looking up at the trees. I'm going, he repeated, and the sound was more of an echo than a question or an answer.

Langue entre-temps (6)

Je partais encore et toujours. Comme si ça pouvait être aussi simple. Ce n'est pas toujours simple. C'est le monde dans lequel je vis : j'ai essayé de tout mettre dans un seul cadre. Il est essentiel de se rappeler que nous n'exprimons jamais toute la vérité. En ton absence, je me demande : si j'étais restée ; si j'étais passée à autre chose ; si je m'étais dit de laisser l'histoire se terminer ; si j'avais appris à dépasser la distance ; à dépasser le poids des faits. Dans l'obscurité de toutes ces petites villes, je m'interroge.

Language in the Meanwhile (6)

I was always and already leaving. Like it could be that simple. It's hardly simple sometimes. This is the world I live in: I tried to fit it all inside one frame. It is crucial to remember that we never express the whole truth. In absence, I wonder: what if I'd stayed; if I'd moved on; if I told myself to let the story end; if I learned to move beyond the distance; to move beyond outweighing the facts. In the darkness of all these small towns, I wonder.

I started writing lots of letters before college; before I left home. I don't know why I was drawn to letter-writing. I don't know why I've been drawn to any of the things or people I've been drawn to in my life, but one summer a close friend left home and we began writing letters to each other. Those letters, though I didn't know it at the time, were my real education. Once, when my friend was in a city somewhere and I was in college in the Hudson Valley, he wrote to ask how I was doing. In reply, I reproduced the Linda Gregg poem "Growing Up":

> I am reading Li Po. The TV is on
> with the sound off.
> I've seen this movie before.
> I turn on the sound for just a moment
> when the man says, "I love you."
> Then turn it off again and go on reading.

That was all I sent my friend in reply.

I never could let that poem go. It was my stasis; my return to normalcy after every cycle of turmoil I brought on myself, because I did always bring them on myself. I didn't know that at the time, but I know it now. Whenever anyone asked me how I was doing, I would first think to myself, *I am reading Li Po...* It's not that I was always reading Li Po, or that I even read Li Po all that often. It was the cold simplicity, the private clarity of Linda Gregg's lines that so aptly described how it felt to live alone, silently re-living—not living—my life's stories.

I turn the stories back on in my mind—*I've seen this before*. I know when the turning point will happen. I know all about the silence afterwards.

Where I grew up in the Hudson Valley, my life was like the seasons, the mountains—a recognizable shape; a return to familiarity, folding within. It was a place to be young, an open wound; midnight swimming and star-gazing and nothing else to do but read books and look at the moon. It wasn't a place for me to grow old. The Hudson Valley: it's a pale green, a navy blue, a corduroy comfort, a knit strength, but I don't live there anymore and rarely go back.

When I left the experiment of trying to be with someone, I left silently, except for that Linda Gregg poem. It was my only farewell utterance. I thought it said everything I was trying to express about why I couldn't be with that person, or rather, why I wasn't fit to be with anyone. I didn't want my ex to take it personally. I knew how one was supposed to love—a generous action, not an indecisive wound. I watched him love me graciously, but I watched from a distance. I could never get closer. That's what I wanted to convey when

I left "Growing Up" taped to the refrigerator door. I don't know how it was received.

My handwriting on the page becomes smaller, scrawnier, whenever I am writing a story I do not wish to tell, or find it hard to tell, or believe, for whatever reason, that something negative might befall me if I tell it. I feel compelled to tell the story of all that happened, but I don't know how to tell stories. Besides, it hasn't ended yet. I'm afraid of writing myself into an ending.

Langue entre-temps (7)

Au fil des ans, j'ai écrit différentes versions (plus poétiques, plus fictionnelles) de cette histoire sur toi. Tu n'existes même pas, pas de la façon dont je t'ai écrit. Tu étais beaucoup de personnes et de sentiments différents ; des expériences ; un schéma d'attachement au désir plutôt qu'à la présence. J'ai pensé qu'en t'écrivant de cette façon, je pourrais m'éloigner de ma nostalgie naturelle, afin de voir clairement l'histoire. Mais ce n'est pas une histoire, c'est une exploration d'un sentiment compliqué. Et s'il y a quelque chose que j'ai déjà en abondance, c'est la distance.

Language in the Meanwhile (7)

Over the years, I've written different (more poeticized, more fictionalized) versions of this story about you. You don't even exist—not in the way I'm writing you. You were many different people and feelings; experiences; a pattern of attaching myself to longing instead of presence. I thought that writing you this way might help me gain some distance from my habit of longing, in order to see the story clearly. But this isn't a story—it's an exploration of a complicated feeling. And if there's one thing I already have in abundance, it is distance.

I've been teaching writing to undergraduates as part of my degree. I like the work; it suits me. Anonymous faces arrive in my classroom in the city, fresh from the strip malls and cornfields of the suburbs and prairies. I'm good at drawing them out of themselves—discovering their fears, and joys, and hesitancies. They leave my classroom three months later three inches taller, no longer unrecognizable to themselves. Through writing, they touch the core of something—startle themselves into being in the face of a mirror. They confront the azure skies above and the puddles of mire below, and one is never the same after trudging through puddles. It's not that I want to depress them or be the instigator of their young adult depression. And I feel more than a little culpable when, here and there, one or two of them turn down a darker path. I don't want to take away their happiness just because I myself am often unhappy. I simply want them to gain the skills of awareness, observation, analysis, and self-understanding.

The trouble is, in pursuit of these things, there can be so much uncertainty.

My students are sleepwalkers when they come to me. By the time they leave, they are scientists of mystery. I don't know how writing sparks this transformation. Perhaps on some level I do know. Perhaps I've taught them well. Or maybe they would undergo this transformation still without me. Maybe it has only to do with youth and maturity, and not with writing at all. I don't know. And I'm a little old-fashioned; a bit of a luddite—by choice, but also by necessity. I'm often broke, I can't afford to pay for Internet at home, so I grade all their papers at the café. It's become a running joke with all my students: they tell me they'll send in their essays by carrier pigeon. Did you get my smoke signal? they ask when they walk in. I sent it last night from the top of the Hancock building. Is this a candle wax dripping? they tease when I hand back their papers. Don't tell me you forgot your quill today!

They tease me for my letter-writing tattoo. It's a drawing of a man placing a letter in a USPS box which I got with Alex at the end of the year he lived here. He has it on his arm, and I have it on mine. The man in the drawing is Ted Berrigan, popular poet from the second wave of the New York School in the '60s. It's not so much that I love Berrigan's poems, although I do like them, especially *Train Ride*. It was the letter and the postal box that hooked me; the act of sending, and the possibility of response.

The drawing was by George Schneeman, an artist from the New York School group who had illustrated some of Berrigan's books and drawn a lot of fliers for the readings at St. Mark's Church. I attended a dinner full of poets last year, and someone who knew Ted's son, Anselm, took a picture of my tattoo and sent it to him. Ted was dead by then, but

Anselm was in California that night. Anselm wrote back and said he thought it was nice, or maybe funny, or maybe both. When I wasn't around poets, just walking down the street, strangers grabbed my arm and asked me if I worked for the postal service. I've never worked for the postal service. And I don't live in California or anywhere near St. Mark's. I live in Chicago, near Carl Sandburg's former home on the north side. I like Carl Sandburg's poems. I like the one about Chicagoans sturdily facing the winter with their hearts in their throats. I may live alone, but I live alone in the city of Chicago, where no one lets the wind swallow them whole.

This fall, I've been making the sleepwalkers in my class write letters. I told them to find a real notebook, not a tablet or iPad. They have to handwrite, I told them. You'll think differently, I said, better that way. Each week they write a letter to a Person, Place, Feeling, or Concept: Dear Isaac; Dear Hudson Valley; Dear Loneliness; Dear Solipsism. Some days when the weather is nice, I bring them outdoors and scatter them in the grass to write their letters. I plant myself in one spot where they can find me when they're finished and write letters along with them, but only in my head: Dear Isaac, I'm sorry I couldn't love you; Dear Hudson Valley, I'm sorry I couldn't stay; Dear Loneliness, you never told me you would be an added layer to my choice; Dear Solipsism, teach me what I can know.

People born on the day of my birth are said to have creative ability; a poetic sensibility. They're said to know what they want out of life, yet they struggle to make a decision. In love, we tend to put the other first—to our detriment sometimes. We spread ourselves thin. We want a long-term love but the reality becomes too disappointing. Why did I give up so much for the other? I still ask myself sometimes. Little things, but the small things meant everything to me.

Little things, like the list I found in a journal from high school called Things that Are Good: fridge magnet poetry, flannel shirts, green tea, short stories, found text, found sounds, found objects + images, sharing ideas, meeting people, writing, sweaters, movies that make me think, wearing boots that belonged to my father, shawls that belonged to my mother, autumn leaves, Marc Chagall, sending mail, receiving mail, listening to someone play banjo through the wall, Egon Schiele, underlining passages in books, James Joyce, Oscar Wilde, finding beauty in the everyday, Mark Rothko, Merce Cunningham, staying up all night, rivers and bridges.

Or the same list I made at the end of college: lying naked beneath white sheets, wind blowing through the house, living surrounded by trees and wildflowers in the mountains, cooking dinner very late at night, growing up by living on your own, teaching your heart to breathe, teaching your feet to step firmly on stones, teaching your head to love this quiet.

Langue entre-temps (8)

J'ai beaucoup de temps pour penser. Il y a si peu de distractions. Je suis bien seule. J'essaie donc de donner du sens à tous les endroits où j'ai vécu et voyagé ; pourquoi j'ai aimé ou détesté chacun d'entre eux ; pourquoi les aimer et les haïr m'a empêché d'y vivre vraiment ; pourquoi je quitte des endroits, même ceux que j'aime ; pourquoi suis-je une personne qui déserte. « Dieu sait combien de villes, de quartiers, de cimetières, de ponts et de passages j'ai traversés. » (Rilke). J'ai toujours l'impression de me soustraire à une image dès qu'elle commence à se fixer, comme si j'avais peur d'être captive d'un lieu d'où je ne pourrais me replier.

Language in the Meanwhile (8)

I have a lot of time to think. There are so few distractions. I'm quite alone. So I'm trying to make sense of all the places I've lived and traveled; why I loved or hated each one; why loving and hating them kept me from really living in them; why I leave places, even the places I love; why I am a person who leaves. "Heaven only knows through how many cities, districts, cemeteries, bridges and alleyways." (Rilke). It always seems as though I retreat from an image as soon as it is beginning to solidify—as if I am afraid of being caught in a place from which I cannot withdraw.

Isaac. He's hardly real to me now. He was hardly real to me then. But we did live together for three years after college in the Hudson Valley, before I left him and moved to Chicago for graduate school. Our place was so small it left no room for us to be separate people. There was no room for his instruments, so we stuffed them between the bookshelves and the couch. My desk became the dumping ground for keys, coins, sweaters, and receipts, so I stopped writing. My internal monologue disappeared. On the surface, we had a nice time together: we went to the movies, where we didn't need to speak; we drank silent beers at local bars while watching basketball games, though I've never liked sports; we walked home at night past lush and fertile gardens planted by people who I imagined had spacious rooms inside where they could be themselves, where they could recognize themselves.

    My own garden, planted on the porch with Isaac, had been filled with all my favorites: basil, rosemary, mint, oregano, and pea shoots climbing up the railing. We joked that we would yet survive the winter. But the sun was blocked by the roof of a neighboring home, and every plant withered away and died—even the mint, a plant that is famously sturdy. The purple flowers of the oregano turned brown and quietly tucked themselves inside the pot. I didn't know how to think about anything anymore. I felt alone with Isaac always. I think he felt alone with me too.

He thought I was bored every time I was silent, which was often. He often wanted to go camping, and I often wanted to read at home. My silence made me happy: in my silence, I knew exactly what I was. But my silence made Isaac nervous, and unhappy. He thought I wasn't interested in what he had to say, or in the activity we were sharing. But I wasn't bored exactly. I don't know. I just wasn't there. I looked around: I couldn't see myself anywhere.

That's what I told myself when I left. It was probably more complicated than that. Sometimes you have to get what you want in order to realize how little you want it.

Isaac had called once, a few months after I left. I was on the phone with my sister and missed his call.

I'm on the phone, I wrote in a text while I continued listening to my sister talk on speakerphone. I'll call back in a few, I said. I called back in a few, but he didn't pick up.

I'm free now, I wrote in a text, if you want to talk.

It's not a good time, he replied.

You called me, I said out loud to the empty room.

Langue entre-temps (9)

Parfois, quand je suis seule dans mon appartement, j'ai l'impression que tu es là avec moi. Je fais bouillir de l'eau pour le thé ou je coupe des légumes dans la cuisine, et pendant un instant, j'ai l'impression de te voir du coin de l'œil, en train de lire sur le divan dans l'autre pièce. Et plus tard, je lirai dans le fauteuil, recroquevillée à la lueur d'une lampe, et je lirai quelque ligne de poésie ou une phrase dans un livre et je l'entendrai avec ta voix, ou je verrai ton visage penché sur ton texte, tes cheveux tombant sur tes yeux. Je te verrai assis là, du coin de mon regard. Quand je me tourne complétement vers toi, je vois que tu n'es pas vraiment là, mais je sens malgré tout ta présence.

Language in the Meanwhile (9)

Sometimes when I am home in my apartment alone, I feel as though you're there with me. I'll be boiling water for tea or chopping vegetables in the kitchen, and for a moment I'll think I see you in the corner of my eye, reading on the couch in the other room. And later I'll be reading in the armchair, curled up in lamplight, and I'll read some line of poetry or a sentence in a book and hear it in your voice, or see your face bent over your own copy, your hair falling in your eyes. I'll see you sitting there, in the corner of my vision. When I turn to face you fully I see that you're not really there, but still I feel your presence.

When I sleep, I sleep with my secrets at the foot of the bed. I don't often dream. But the other night, I was too warm in sleep. I dreamt of Paris, but Paris was a mountain range, and it was upside down. Or maybe I was. I was standing with my feet squeezed between two boulders. A chatterbox girl I'd worked with once was there. Her words were spinning all around me. Somewhere behind me was the Eiffel Tower, alerting me that this was definitely Paris, but it looked an awful lot like the Hudson Valley. My head was surrounded by air. I'm certain I was upside down. I could tell that I wanted to be there. But there were too many words, too many sentences. I was getting swallowed up in them. That wasn't how I wanted to be.

It would be foolish for a translator to mix the two methods of translation: foreignization and domestication. In foreignization, you bring the reader toward the writer. In domestication, you bring the writer toward the reader.

If I erased the unfamiliarity of the original text, to help my readers understand me, I would instigate colossal misunderstanding. The meaning lies in the context behind the words: if I change the context to a more palatable scene for my English-speaking audience, I will be changing what the scene effectively means.

Some nights when I am out with friends, drinking at a bar or someone's house or out for karaoke, I reach a point where I become unable to speak. It has nothing to do with drink or with fatigue, even if I have had too much to drink or am fatigued. Instead, it is a failure of my language to match the mental state that I am in. On these nights, I tell my friends that I am stepping outside for a cigarette and will be back in five minutes. Then I put on my jacket, step out into the street, and head toward home.

I told Isabelle I had to set aside the translation for the rest of spring while I finished my thesis. I am always getting ahead of myself, rushing on to the next idea, and my advisor reminded me that I needed to pace myself. But Isabelle and I continued to talk while the project was on pause. I'd grown attached to her. Talking to Isabelle had filled the space that opened up when Alex left Chicago, and I think she felt similarly.

The only thing we never talked about was where they were now; what they were doing; who they were with since they were not with us; how large or small a role they played in our current lives, as if the version of them we were writing and translating had become more real than who they were in actuality. Isabelle had written about this too, in her book—how she was starting to forget some details about her Alex. *J'ai oublié quel sorte de chaussures tu portes*, she wrote: I've forgotten what kind of shoes you wear.

I'd forgotten what kind of shoes my Alex wore too, and often questioned whether I had ever known; if I'd ever paid close enough attention. I'd often only seen what I wanted to see—excellent quality for a writer, poor practice for a person in the world. But then, people who read James Joyce and Anaïs Nin when they are young have a hard time being a Person later on.

A Person: Alex and I always capitalized certain words when we wanted to Emphasize their Meaning, the way the old Romantic poets had done. How to Be a Person was the title of an assignment I gave my students last year at the end of term. They'd been reading Fernando Pessoa ('pessoa' = 'person' in Portuguese) and taking night walks through the city with their hands cupped around their eyes to Emphasize the way in which they see. *Un essai merveilleux*, Isabelle said; a wonderful endeavor, a wonderful essay. The prompt was an idea I'd had on one of my night walks with Alex. Back then, he'd said he wanted to read what my students wrote about their walks, but by the time they wrote them we were hardly speaking anymore, so I never sent them. "How much of the world passes me by each day without me noticing?" one of them wrote.

This was the plan: to finish my thesis on 17th to 19th-century French female letter-writers, then spend the summer after graduation in France. My translation professor had helped me apply to a residency in the northeast—a two-and-a-half-hour train ride from Paris. I would stay in Isabelle's spare room the first month so we could work together, then go on to the residency for the rest of the summer. Isabelle was letting me stay for free—*ce n'est pas la mer à boire*, she said; it's not a big deal, it's not as if you have to drink the sea—and I had enough savings to pay for the residency where all my meals, lodging, laundry, everything was included. I looked at photos of the château online every day, counting the days.

The château had changed hands several times through sales, dowries, inheritances, and occupancies, including by the Nazis in the early 1940s. But the original ownership could be traced back to the family of Denis Diderot. The château had been the home of Diderot's daughter, Marie-Angélique, in the 1700s. It's romantic nowadays to think about Diderot as a bohemian and the black sheep of the family line, but the fact remains that his family was ashamed of him. Despite being known as what we'd call today a fuckboi, he did marry—a woman he'd loved in his youth—but the marriage was not a happy one. I imagine his daughter wasn't pleased with his lifestyle (can I blame her? How would I feel if my famous father cheated on my mom?), which would explain why she hid all of Diderot's papers in the château. The unpublished manuscripts would not be unearthed until some time after his death by then-proprietor Baron Charles Levavasseur, who authorized their official publication in 1830.

The essay I still had to write for my thesis was on Diderot's love affair and correspondence with a woman ten years younger than him: Sophie Volland. By the time he met her, he was 43 years old. She was part of the Paris bourgeoisie but kept a summer home in Isle-sur-Marne—an hour's drive today from the château in Orquevaux. Sophie and Diderot were together for thirty years, until their death. They died within a few days of each other.

At times I talked about translation, on a basic level, with my undergraduate students. Several came from homes where they spoke more than one language. But even then, they were used to quickly translating basic meaning from one language to the other in their head. They hadn't thought much about the gaps, failures, losses, and impossibilities that come with writing down a literary translation. They heard 'translation' and thought 'transliteration,' imagining that, as John Ciardi has said, each word in Language A would equal each word in Language B.

I would talk with them about how language is created based on the way the people who use it think, eat, cook, work, and generally behave in their world and that, as my students probably knew by now, these practices are different the world over.

I'm sure many adults have told you that all humans are the same, I said. It's their way of motivating you to be kind to everyone you meet. But the truth is that we are not the same, and that our differences define us for who we are.

Can't kindness still play a role in things, though? one student asked.

It has been estimated that Diderot wrote more than 500 letters to Sophie, but only 137 had been found at the time of their first printing. Fifty more were found by the Baron after that, hidden in the château with the rest of his papers. None of Sophie's letters have been found.

I find myself troubled by this. I find myself imagining the potential route of her letters to destruction's door. If her letters ended up in the hands of Diderot's daughter at Orquevaux, perhaps instead of burying them along with Diderot's papers, she burned them in a fit of anger toward her father's affair. When I began looking into the story of Sophie and Diderot, I assumed that Sophie's letters had not survived for the same reason that so many women's stories have been erased—because a man did not find them important enough to save. The possibility that a woman erased another woman's history is more upsetting. Even if Marie-Angélique was hurting, I wish that she had been able to see the love between her father and Sophie for what it was—a love of truth, and of equality. "Look within yourself, my Sophie," Diderot wrote in one of his letters, "and tell me why you are so sincere, so frank, so true in your words? It's because these very qualities are the foundation of your character and the guide of your behavior."

Sophie's given name was Louise-Henriette. No photographs of her have ever surfaced. 'Sophie' was the name that Diderot gave her because it meant 'wisdom.' The only physical description of her that I've ever been able to find was a scant Wikipedia article that claimed she had small, dry hands and little, watery eyes. Sophie with the poor eyesight; Sophie with the small, dry hands. I liked that Diderot loved her not for her beauty, which scholars seem to claim she did not have, but for her intellect, sincerity, and curiosity. Not that her supposed lack of beauty kept them from engaging in the physical, as all evidence in Diderot's letters proves that they loved each other in every way: "How are you today? Did you sleep well? Do you sometimes sleep as I do, open-armed. How tender was your gaze yesterday! How you've been looking at me like that for quite a while…" An article I found said that Diderot loved Sophie because she understood him—and because she loved him back, *à la folie*.

Langue entre-temps (10)

Je préfère l'histoire se cachant juste en dessous de l'histoire. Je me demande toujours pourquoi. C'est ainsi que se passe l'errance. C'est très lent.

Language in the Meanwhile (10)

I prefer the story hiding just beneath the story. I am always wondering why. That's the way the wandering goes. It's very slow.

Researchers love to fill the silent gaps of history. A French professor at a prestigious university on the East Coast recently published an article claiming to have discovered the lost letters of Sophie Volland. But I fear she wrote for the wrong audience: the work was pure historical fiction, containing a preface in the voice of her own persona as editor—a kind of introduction to the work you're about to see. This is another classic move from 17th to 19th-century French literature: the fictional preface in the voice of a humble editor who has "just stumbled upon" this long-lost, long sought-after work.

The researcher's preface was followed by a few fictional letters she wrote herself in the voice of Sophie. I've read the preface closely but only skimmed the letters: when you spend so much time thinking about a person whose voice you will never hear (or never hear again) you develop your own idea of what their voice must sound like. It has very little to do with them and everything to do with you. I found I could not spend much time reading the professor's historical fiction disguised as scholarship because her Sophie was different from my Sophie, and I believed—however foolishly—that my Sophie was more true.

Alex had left Chicago by the time I pinned down the focus of my thesis, and this was just as well. When he was with me, I felt more myself than when I was alone or away from him—my mind sharper; my thoughts clearer, more urgent. But I had targeted all my energy toward him, reserving little for my family and friends, much less for any other practical task I had to complete: cooking, cleaning, grocery shopping, budgeting in order to pay my bills. Now that he was gone, I found myself exhausted all the time. I couldn't muster the desire for anything. I had spent all my energy with him—for him—and now I was without him.

There was something highly impractical about Alex that I loved and resented at the same time. I loved that he didn't think too much about tasks like taking out the trash or buying refills of laundry detergent before he ran out. It meant that every day was lived in the service of literature, and poetry, and ideas, and aesthetics. But I equally resented him for all of this. I resented him for barely being able to take care of himself. I resented having to bring him half of whatever I'd cooked for myself the night before because he barely knew how to feed himself. I would schlep an extra Tupperware to campus where I'd sometimes find him in the morning in sweatpants, drinking an espresso with bags under his eyes. He was always vague about what he'd been doing the night before, and though he always made an effort to imply that he'd been writing or studying, I knew it was more likely a question not of what he'd been doing but who.

And he never told me. Not a single time did he tell me about anyone he'd been with, or wanted to be with, or thought about being with in the past, present, or future, though I thought it likely he had slept his way through the campus. As often as I was able to find him randomly in some hallway at school or on the benches in the square in our neighborhood, he would also disappear for long periods of time and then return, as if the disappearance had never happened. It would be at night, or during a long Saturday or Wednesday afternoon, and I would feel sick to my stomach while doing laundry or taking out the trash or boxing up some stir-fry I knew I would end up bringing to school for him, thinking about who he was sleeping with and where; if they had books in their apartments, or if they didn't read at all; how he could sleep with someone who didn't read or own books; if he looked at them with the same flirtatious, witty smirk he gave me, but if, with them, it was genuinely flirtatious; and why, if Diderot the black sheep, Diderot the fuckboi bohemian, could love Sophie with the watery eyes, Sophie with the small, dry hands, why couldn't Alex, why wouldn't I get an answer as to why Alex *ne pouvait pas m'aimer*.

Langue entre-temps (11)

Cet après-midi, je me suis promenée dans la rue, les chevilles nues, afin de faire des courses pour le dîner que je vais préparer ce soir. Les branches des arbres semblaient massives et noires par-dessus l'étendue bleu clair du ciel. Le sol brun et hivernal révélait des reflets verts. Ce soir, je ferai une soupe avec des saucisses, du chou frisé, des carottes et des pommes de terre. Je vais couper l'oignon jaune et espérer que ce soir il ne me fasse pas pleurer. Je vais laisser mijoter la soupe sur le feu jusqu'à ce qu'elle soit prête. Je vais griller deux moitiés de baguette au four, face en l'air, avec du beurre. Je laisserai les rideaux ouverts pendant que je mange. Ce soir, je ne ressens aucun désir en dehors de moi-même et de ma vie bien rangée. C'est une bénédiction ; je me sens soulagée dans ces petits moments où je n'ai pas envie d'avoir de tes nouvelles. Cela me fait penser que ceci pourrait suffire - ces baguettes, ces promenades, le visage d'un ami cher qui apparaît à la fenêtre. Comment ne pas se contenter de cette vie, mais plutôt de la célébrer.

Language in the Meanwhile (11)

This afternoon I walked down the street with my ankles bare to shop for groceries for the dinner I'll make tonight. The branches of the trees looked strong and black against the clear blue expanse of the sky. The brown, long-wintered ground showed hints of green. Tonight I'll make a pot of soup with sausage, kale, carrots, and potatoes. I'll chop the yellow onion and hope that tonight, it does not make me cry. I'll allow the soup to simmer on the stove until it is ready. I'll toast two halves of a baguette in the oven, face up, dripping with butter. I'll leave the curtains open while I eat. Tonight, I feel no longing outside of my self and my own curated life. It's a blessing; I feel relieved in these small moments when I am not longing to hear from you. It makes me think that perhaps this might be enough—these baguettes; these walks; the face of a friend I love appearing in the window. How not to settle for but celebrate this life.

I completed my degree. I walked across the stage with my peers. I stooped and bowed my head so the dean could bestow me with my master's hood, and everyone clapped the way they clapped for everyone else. My parents flew in from the Hudson Valley. My sister was stuck in Manhattan, but my parents passed on the message that she loved me. We took photographs in my cap and gown and ate burgers with some friends of mine and their families. My parents went back home after a day or so of wandering the city, and I began to pack for my summer away.

I'd found a subletter for the summer, another grad student at the school, so I'd be leaving everything in the apartment mostly as it was. I only needed to clear up space for her in the study, the bedroom, and the bathroom. I knew I should pack lightly and not bring too many books or papers. I would need my preferred yellow legal pads for translating, and I thought I might work toward my own book, too— something about language; travel; missed connections; a never-ending search. But searching through my desk drawers for the papers I needed to bring had been distracting: I kept discovering fragments of old writing—terrible stuff, mostly, that never needed to see the light of day—but underneath a small stack of my essays with comments from my workshop classmates, I found a prose poem I'd written when Alex had been here.

We'd gone through a phase, when Alex had been here, of mild obsession with those Missed Connection ads that people post on Craigslist in every city. Many nights we'd sat up late in my living room laughing over all that misplaced desire. A man would try to find a woman he'd seen at the gym, or a woman would try to find a man she'd found attractive on the train. It was all very '90s, very *You've Got Mail*. We'd make predictions about which potential couples were more likely to find each other. We never got so far as to imagine if, after they found each other, they would stay together.

But one night, we created a game: write a prose poem in the form of a Missed Connection ad, and post it on Craigslist. The poem had to include a living room, a percentage, and a river. Then we'd wait to see if anybody found us. My poem nearly wrote itself immediately. It was winter; Alex had been in my life for something like five months or so, and whenever I walked away from him, this poem would slowly write itself for me. I'd never written it down until we decided on the game, but each line seemed to accompany my every footstep. I heard it in my head when I woke up and fell asleep, rode the train, and walked to class. I heard it in my head each time I watched Alex walk away from me.

The game felt dangerous to me because of this, as if Alex had read my thoughts and knew the secret elements of my poem. How could he have known, I thought, as we sat there on my floor, that percentages, a river, and a living room lived inside my secret poem? I told myself it was because he knew me so well—as well as I knew myself. But if he knew me as well as I knew myself, that would mean he knew the feelings I never shared. And if he knew the feelings I never chose to share, that meant the game had been designed to torment me. Come on, he seemed to be saying, tell me your feelings, how hard could it be?

The game felt dangerous, too, because we avoided the topic of whether or not we would read each other's poems. Despite my hesitations about what the game might soon reveal, we had a great laugh while coming up with the idea, and the laughter and the wine we'd been drinking had elevated the mood. Alex went home soon after, saying he had to write his poem right away. I opened the door for him and, after an awkward shuffle with the bottle of wine—no you, please take it, I couldn't, I've had enough—he rushed down the steps, pausing only briefly to look back at me with that familiar smirk before disappearing into the street.

It was me who ended up with the bottle of wine. I sat up on the couch for another hour or so, staring at the ceiling, wondering if Alex was writing his poem at home or if there had been someone he'd run off to meet. I drank a bit more of the wine, then dragged my computer onto my lap to write and post the poem before I could worry over it any longer.

MISSED CONNECTION: Chicago, IL: w4m; SUBJECTS WE LEFT OUT

If I stand back far enough I can see the roads that bring you to the river where you lose yourself, regain footing in a fractured poem. Sometimes I travel no more than 150 square feet each day. We fill the gaps with questions, repeat and answer, until I am traveling your roads and you are patching up my square feet with percentages. If you turned around, you could take the road back to where you came from, and you might like it more there the second time around. Or maybe that is more than I can hope for. I have been lost, and you've been hiding in the corner glancing over. Tell me who was reading that night I tripped over people on the porch to say hello but did not. Tell me where I sat, cross-legged on a living room floor. If you saw me, tell me I was there.

I received two responses the following day when I woke up. The first was from a girl whose name was Mo. She had assumed the ad was real, but guessed my true intentions: she said it sounded like a poem; that it would make a great poem if I added line breaks, or even if I didn't; that it would make a great prose poem too. The second response I received was from another stranger, this time with no name attached. It sounded like a man. There were several typos in several run-on sentences about how sure he was that he was the intended recipient. The end of his reply was this: "What's keeping us from finding one another?" I couldn't help thinking this odd reply was Alex messing with me, throwing in a few typos so I wouldn't recognize him. It would be just his kind of humor. He probably hadn't even written or posted his own poem, only checked the website until he found the one he knew was mine. I was afraid to see him in class that night; afraid that I would be too nervous to speak to him; that I would flush and stammer even if we never brought up the game at all. But his seat was empty when I arrived in class that evening, and the professor mentioned he was sick. I launched myself into the discussion on the prose poems of Francis Ponge, and I didn't hear anything from Alex for 48 hours.

Langue entre-temps (12)

Je ne peux pas exprimer les maintes façons dont certaines personnes restent avec toi.

Language in the Meanwhile (12)

I cannot express how many ways some people stay with you.

I'm not happy right now, the cab driver said, as I dragged my suitcase toward the car in the afternoon heat. I just came from O'Hare just now. There's a lot of traffic right now.

I said nothing as he heaved my suitcase into the trunk. He began the drive out of the city, and I fell asleep as the restaurant signs shifted from English to Spanish. But I woke a few minutes later when I heard the driver saying he was happy I was heading for international departures. Too much traffic in the domestic, he reminded me.

When he asked where I was going, I told him I was traveling to France to work on a book about a translator traveling to France to work on a book. He asked if I would be as good as Stephen King one day, and had I seen Stephen King on Jimmy Kimmel recently, or maybe it was Stephen Colbert? Well, Stephen King had been on the air, and Donald Trump came up, and Stephen King told Stephen Colbert, or maybe it was Jimmy Kimmel, that Trump had blocked him—

him, Stephen King!—on Twitter. The audience laughed. Jimmy Kimmel, or maybe it was Stephen Colbert, asked Stephen King what he'd said on Twitter that made Donald Trump decide to block him, but Stephen King said he didn't remember.

Have you seen this film called *Misery*? the driver asked me. It's called *Misery*. I think it's Stephen King. It's about a writer who goes to the mountains to work on a book. He gets injured in the snow and a woman finds him and nurses him back to health. But when he starts to get well again and tells the woman that it's time for him to go home, the woman breaks both his legs to make him stay. That's where the film gets weird and creepy, the driver said. I think it's like a drama. I think it's Stephen King. It's called *Misery*—look it up, put it in the Google.

Miiii–ser–yyyy, he drawled, staring into my eyes in the rearview mirror.

Langue entre-temps (13)

C'est samedi, et la journée entière s'offre à moi dans un bain de lumière. Je me suis réservé toute la journée pour n'écrire qu'à toi ; pour m'immerger dans ce monde que j'ai inventé sur toi. Je m'ouvre à toi, je pose le son de l'émerveillement de mon âme devant cette projection de toi.

Je sors sur le balcon pour fumer une cigarette, et quand je rentre à l'intérieur et que je regarde dans le miroir, je m'aperçois qu'une trace de cendre s'est déposée sur ma joue. Je cherche partout le moindre scintillement de toi. Je regarde dans le silence, dans l'abîme de l'ignorance de mon cœur. J'écris davantage quand je m'adresse à toi : à ton absence, à notre silence et à notre distance. Peut-être que l'écriture n'est qu'une longue et lente découverte de l'adresse - dévoilant la carte du silence qui a été tracée pour toi.

Language in the Meanwhile (13)

It's Saturday, and the whole day spreads out before me in a wash of light. I've given myself the whole day to write only to you; to immerse myself in this world I've invented of you. I open myself to you; I lay the sound of my soul's wondering before this projection of you.

I go out to the balcony to smoke a cigarette, and when I come back inside and look in the mirror, I see that a trace of ash has settled on my cheek. I look everywhere for the smallest flicker of you. I look in the silence, in the gap of my heart's unknowing. I write most when I address my writing to you: to your absence; to our silence and distance. Maybe writing is only a long, slow discovery of address—unfolding the map of silence that's been laid out for you.

I'd only been to France once before, on a school trip when I was twelve—the year I started learning French and calling myself Isabelle. We ate escargot and baguettes with camembert. I made a big scene about eating the snails: they were drowned in pesto, I think; I'd never eaten pesto before either. I thought all of it was green and gross and slimy. We traveled to Tours, Rouen, Mont Saint-Michel. Most of the photographs I took on disposable cameras came out completely gray and blurred—unsalvageable. Other kids from the trip promised to send me copies of their photos, sharp and clear, but they never did, or I never got them.

In my travel journal, all I wrote about was drama: my crushes on Paul and John; our middle-school flirting, which was really just teasing, playing games. "Saw Notre Dame today," I wrote at the end of a particularly drama-filled entry, "but now I'm too tired to tell you about it."

We wrote our names in Sharpie on the top of the Eiffel Tower one night, where John said he hoped he would propose to someone someday—carry her up the stairs and, once they reached the top, ask her to spend the rest of her life with him. We were twelve. John was thinking about marriage. I was probably thinking about camembert.

We visited the Musée d'Orsay, Champs Élysées, le Bon Marché, the Mona Lisa in the Louvre—how small that painting is. It's like admiring your grandmother's towering stature when you're young, then growing up to see her sunken in a wheelchair. We rode a tourist boat down the Seine and sat across from a couple who were performatively making out. We must have been loud with our astonishment—we were pretty sheltered East Coast kids. They laughed at us and said, You're in France now! Get used to it!

There was a sex shop and, above that, a hostel or apartment building across the street from our hotel. I couldn't tell the difference back then between temporary and permanent places for living. Some older teenage boys spotted me and my classmates from their window in the indeterminate building. One of them shouted, Hey! Do you want to see my ass? then dropped his pants and shoved his bare ass out the window.

It occurs to me now that, as a bunch of stupid American kids, we assumed, because we were in France, everyone around us must be French. But maybe that couple on the boat was from Barcelona, or Naples. I remember the ass guy's accent so clearly. I think he was German.

Isabelle would be at work the afternoon I arrived in Paris, so we agreed that I would wait for her at a café in the neighborhood nearby. That was fine with me; I didn't want to drag my suitcase around the city, and I knew I would be tired from the flight. But when I got out of the cab outside the café, I saw a pink neon advertisement for palm readings next door—a sign for Psychic Madam Eva. I'd never had my palm read before. I'd always been curious but hesitant. I gave the cab driver 40 euros in cash and maneuvered my bags through Madam Eva's door. At the sight of my bags, Madam Eva knew I was a tourist, or maybe only tourists ever visited her shop. At any rate, she spoke to me in English. She sat me down and got right to the point: I want you to think of two wishes, she said. Keep one to yourself and share one with me. Then give me the hand you write with.

  Privately, I wished that one day I would be less governed by skepticism; that one day I would find the strength to say what I wanted to say.

I'd like for things to work out with my writing, I said aloud, holding out my right hand. She looked at my palm for a moment, then directly in my eyes as she said with rehearsed clarity, I will have to tell you everything that I see, good and bad. *D'accord?*

I allowed my mind to wander restlessly as Madam Eva searched my palm for something to say. Her fingers were cold, but in the summer heat, I didn't mind.

I see that you are a person who keeps to yourself, Madam Eva said.

I tried to let my face convey little feeling.

You want to connect, she said. You know there are people out there who care, but you keep yourself hidden from them.

You should not do this, she said. There are people waiting out there.

Aussi, she said, after another few moments of searching, I see that you are looking for a significant other. There is a person, she said, you for some time have had feelings for, but you have not told them. You should not be afraid, she said, her eyes trying hard to catch mine. You should tell them your feelings, she said. They have feelings too.

Maybe it was just the differences in the sentence constructions of our languages, but I found it telling that Madam Eva did not say, They have feelings *for you.*

In the café, while drinking an espresso with a small butter cookie and waiting for Isabelle, I remembered a conversation I'd had with my friend James a month or so after Alex moved back to Florence. James and I had gone for drinks at Moody's in Edgewater. He met me at the tattoo shop down the street, just as the artist was finishing the final jagged line of a drawing from *The Savage Detectives*. We walked over to the bar in the summer heat, my right thigh wrapped in cellophane below my shorts. James ordered us two or three rounds of local beers and we chain-smoked at a table at the back of the patio. We talked about Visceral Realism and the real Infrarealists of the '70s, and the foggy confusion infused in the atmosphere of Latin American literature. We wondered if we had been our own kind of Visceral Realists before, when we first met at the start of grad school; back when we drank more often and ran around with a rowdy group of poets united by impulse more than any single literary aesthetic.

James asked which character I was from the Visceral Realists in the book and I said María Font, because I like so many different kinds of art, and because I like to have people show up at my house unannounced to read poems or talk about nothing; and because, like her, I'm kind of into rough sex, but also, like her, you wouldn't know that at first, because most of the time I look as though I couldn't give a shit. Summer does this to me especially. As we talked, I felt groggy. Carrying the weight of my head around felt like a victory.

So what else is new? James asked. Still fucking that PhD from German Studies?

I made a face, then sipped my beer.

Not if I can help it, I said. James laughed and leaned back in his seat, exhaling smoke from the cigarette he'd bummed from me, then reached forward again for his beer.

Still hung up on Florence Boy? he replied.

I stubbed my cigarette out in the ashtray and told him about a dream I'd had that week in which I got back together with a few ex-boyfriends. In each scene, I wore the pleasant smile acquired while dating them—an acquiescence to the possibility of this or that life. In the dream's third act, I flew to Florence where Alex was living once again. On the way, I lost my backpack in Seattle, and when I got to Florence— instead of seeing Alex, or even telling him I was there—I turned around and went back home, stopping in the Pacific Northwest to search for my baggage.

Well, James said. You like your intimacy at a distance.

I adjusted the cellophane on my thigh and changed the subject back to Bolaño, telling James I'd started reading *2666* but wasn't sure if I liked it or not, because I missed the first-person intimacy of *The Savage Detectives*, although I know Bolaño wrote *2666* just before he died, so maybe he was feeling more removed from things.

It's a bit depressing when you think about it, isn't it? I asked James. How the most radical poets all get fat and lonely in the end, taking pills and drinking chamomile tea instead of coffee or beer, though they still don't know how to wash their clothes or clean their houses?

In tenth grade French class, I watched the film *Amélie* for the first time. The teacher fast-forwarded through the father's sperm swimming across the screen and the fifteen couples with their simultaneous orgasms, but I watched the film again later on my own. I've probably seen it about fifteen times by now, maybe more. The plot of the movie is spun into action by the discovery of a treasure box in the wall of Amélie's apartment. In her mission to return the box to its owner, she transforms from a shy and lonely introvert who lives only inside her imagination into a person on the hunt for unknowable truths about love and understanding; for patterns that cohere into clear facts. Although patterns aren't really Amélie's realm so much as Nino's—her love interest in the film, another seeker of truth. While Amélie is enchanted by the coherence of life's random occurrences, Nino collects patterns: footprints; recordings of unconventional laughs; torn photo-booth images; other odd, intangible things. Of course, the film becomes a love story between them. But I've often thought that once they dropped their performances and saw each other in the full light of reality, instead of elaborately staging each and every moment, they would realize they couldn't fulfill each other as much as they thought they could. Amélie would grow annoyed with Nino's incessant pattern-seeking; Nino would find Amélie's naïve scavenger-hunting tiresome in the end. Or they'd both remain too preoccupied with their own imaginations to give the time and attention to their relationship that it would need in order to thrive. But the movie ends before their relationship even begins, and anyway, what do I know, I live alone.

On Thursday nights in Chicago, a bunch of us would hang out on James and Leslie's porch to drink wine and smoke cigarettes and talk about poetry. The week we'd talked at Moody's, I leafed through a dossier James gave me from the *Chicago Review of Books* about the Infrarealists—how they'd wanted to change the face of Latin American poetry; how they considered themselves revolutionaries, and they were, but they were also just a bunch of rowdy teens and twenty-somethings who caused a disturbance at readings by throwing shit in the face of Octavio Paz.

Everyone went on drinking wine and smoking cigarettes and spliffs and talking about poetry on the porch, and there was food I think; someone brought out bowls of something the way they always do. As midnight approached and we drained all the bottles of wine, we pulled books from the shelves in the living room and read aloud.

I read from the end of "Leave It All Once More," Bolaño's Infrarealist manifesto:

Risk is always elsewhere.
The true poet is the one who is always abandoning himself.

When I got back to my neighborhood that night, I sat on the bench where I used to sit with Alex below the tree in the lamplit square; the light of an elsewhere. I thought about Bolaño, and his best friend, Mario Santiago Papasquiaro, who Bolaño called Ulises Lima when he transformed him into a character in his novel. I thought about the real María Font, whose name was Mara Larrosa, who wrote the most beautifully abstract letters I am ever likely to see. But it would also be true to say that, there in the lamplit square, while smoking and looking up between the branches of the tree, I thought about nothing.

Langue entre-temps (14)

Je n'arrête pas de me retrouver ici. Je ne sais pas quelle en sera la signification.

Language in the Meanwhile (14)

I keep finding myself here. Don't know what its significance will be.

Sometimes it frustrates me that Rilke turned his notebook-novel about his young life in Paris into fiction. The best parts of this novel are the observations and reflections that came from his personal diary. I would have liked to read that book unfiltered.

    The English translator for the edition that I own had this to say:

> Poetry was the stuff of life to [Rilke], and it is astonishing to think of him writing a novel at all, even an anti-novel like *The Notebooks of Malte Laurids Brigge*—so astonishing, in fact, that it might be aptest to think of the work as a long prose poem.

Part of me agrees with this, as I would like for prose to be considered closer to poetry than it often is by scholars and critics, but I also find the statement narrow-minded. I think a writer turns to the form that is the best container for the content, and one could argue that a novel is the best container for a story about a young writer awash in a strange city.

There's another element about prose that I think is very important to consider too, which is more about the larger impulse behind why we are compelled to write it. Think about it: what happens when a writer moves away; leaves home for the first time on their own; abandons everything they've ever known; experiences a jarring rupture in their life so unsettling that it tears apart the boundaries of their writing? I'll tell you what happens: they feel uncertain; they don't know where to go; their boundaries shatter into prose.

Ever since Alex left Chicago, I've been writing letters like this to him in my head. And Alex, the thing I'm learning is that letters give you the freedom to write in every possible genre all at once; to make discoveries you would not encounter if you did not address your writing to an Other; to bring fear and joy and hesitancy and pleasure to the page at the same time.

Rilke knew this too. He would never have written the notebook-novel if he hadn't first written reflective, observational letters about his fears, his joys, his hesitancies, to his wife and to his lover while he was still young and living in that city. He wrote the book not because he knew exactly what he wanted before he began, but because he didn't know. He followed a series of detours, train rides, never-ending searches, hungers, and fears.

What I'm trying to say to you, Alex, is that Rilke wrote the book before he even knew that he was writing it. That's what I've always wanted: to be immersed in the language game. I want to find I've written a book only after I have finished writing it.

My parents hadn't known about the Bolaño tattoo until they came to Chicago for my graduation. We went out to eat at an Italian restaurant on their last night in the city. I was wearing a skirt; my father saw the drawing on my thigh and asked what it signified.

It means different things, I told him. Or, it means different things to different people, depending on the way you look at things.

Like a Rorschach test, he posed.

I guess so, I said. For me it represents a never-ending search leading only to more questions.

The hostess led the three of us to a table.

You know, that's interesting, my father said. We turned sideways to maneuver past the other tables toward our own. I believe in answers, he said, tied up in a neat little bow. How did I birth someone so obsessed with questions?

We laughed, and I told him I did like my home to be tied up in a bow with everything neat and clean and comfortably in its place, so I'm free to go to messy places in my mind.

You have a very complex soul, my mother said, smiling.

We spread butter on our slices of bread and dipped them in a mixture of olive oil, herbs, and grated parmesan cheese.

The challenge, my mother continued, will be finding a partner with a complex soul like yours. You know, someone who can understand you and meet you on that level.

I knew she meant well, but I paused with my bread in the dish.

It's not so easy, I replied. I sipped my wine and checked my phone—no new messages.

Langue entre-temps (15)

Allongés dans le lit cet après-midi, les deux fenêtres ouvertes, les rideaux se soulèvent et se rejoignent. Un vent fort soufflait sur mes membres en-dessous des draps. Je me suis endormie avec la paume de ma main autour de la courbe de l'autre oreiller, imaginant - juste un instant - que c'était ton épaule.

Language in the Meanwhile (15)

Lying in bed this afternoon, both windows open, curtains lifting up and out toward one another. A strong wind rustled over my limbs below the sheets. I fell asleep with my palm around the curve of the extra pillow, imagining—for just a moment—it was your shoulder.

My phone vibrated: a message from Isabelle.

Désolée, ma chérie, I have some things to do, to pick up for us, I'll be a little longer, the traffic from the strike today, *c'est fou !*

Pas de problème, I wrote back, and ordered another coffee.

Si tu veux, she replied, there is a friend nearby with an extra set of keys, I am sending him to you. He will let you in. *À bientôt !*

Isabelle arrived at home as I was unpacking the last of my things and settling into my little room on the mezzanine. Isabelle's bedroom was on the main floor, and my bed was in a loft, up a sturdy wooden ladder, overlooking the living room.

Magnifique ! Isabelle cried when she saw me. *Tu es arrivée !* Her long, thin brown hair was tucked over one shoulder, her bangs slightly windswept against her face. She carried a baguette under her arm and a woven basket full of produce and fresh cheese from the market. I could see a bottle of rosé sticking out of her purse.

Viens en bas ! she waved in a gesture pulling me down the stairs, and I climbed down the ladder to greet her. We kissed each other on the cheeks and hugged tightly. It felt as though I'd come home from a long and difficult time away, though I'd never been there in that place with that person before.

Finish your unpacking and come back down, she said, I will make for us an *apéro. J'éspere que tu aimes le rosé !* she called over her shoulder as she disappeared inside the tiny kitchen.

In college, the girls I lived with used to ask me how I'd slept. It was only well on the mornings they did not ask. I made myself a nest of white to keep dreams out. Dreams felt too close to the world, while I did not. I'd usually wake tired, afraid to place my head back on the pillow. In summer, at our house in the Hudson Valley, spiders crawled in through the door. In autumn, it was ladybugs. By winter, I became well-acquainted with the deer. I liked their quiet and their clean, crisp walk. They would see me and know that I was safe. They would step from the woods into our clearing, and I would give my needs away. I liked the way they never backed down but only stared, as if whispering: I see how you wait for silence to mean something.

The main room of Isabelle's flat was large and spacious for a Parisian apartment near the center of the city, filled with plants, bookshelves, and two oversized windows that opened like doors. Summer nights were long here, and I was glad she had a small balcony for morning coffees and late night eavesdropping on neighbors and passersby below. I was browsing her books when she emerged from the kitchen carrying a tray of sliced baguette, soft cheese, a dish of almonds, thin slices of salami, fresh figs, and two chilled glasses of rosé. She set the tray down on the coffee table and hurried back into the kitchen, returning with the wine bottle in a small bucket of ice.

Asseyez-vous ! she said with mock formality, and we settled into the couch.

We clinked our glasses and I picked a slice of bread with a bit of soft cheese, the bread still warm and the cheese as soft as butter. Isabelle sipped her wine and tucked her feet up on the couch beneath her legs, lightly brushing the gold hoop in her right ear.

Voilà, she said, and looked at me as though we'd known each other since we were very small. *Dis-moi*, she said, tell me everything. I want to know everything.

In the morning, after Isabelle left for work, there was someone I needed to see. I laced up my boots, put my film cameras in my backpack, and set out for a long walk to the Montparnasse Cemetery. I could have taken the metro, but it was my first time in Paris since I was twelve; I wanted to see as much as possible all at once. Isabelle had said we'd go for a walk together by the Canal that evening, so I walked in the other direction through République and past the Pompidou with its long line of tourists stretching down the block. When I reached the Seine and the Pont au Change, I paused for a good long while.

People in Chicago had often asked Alex why he felt he needed to travel in order to translate. With technology bridging the geographical gap, they asked, it's a benefit but not a necessity, no? But Alex always told them the same thing: to see the bridges. To see what they're made of; to see the view from them. To see the way a city washes its language in the river. Only then is it possible to understand the city one is trying to write.

What bridge are you standing on right now, Alex? What bridge is American Alex crossing in New York? I'll tell you the names of the bridges I love, back where I came from: Cortland Street Drawbridge; Dearborn Street Bridge; Franklin Street Bridge; LaSalle Street Bridge; Monroe Street Bridge; Wilson Avenue Bridge; Lyric Opera Bridge. Tell me the names of the bridges you've loved, even if you do not know their names and have to search for them. If you ever see me on one of the bridges you love, tell me I was there.

Langue entre-temps (16)

Pourquoi nous efforçons-nous de nous rapprocher des gens qui ne nous correspondent pas ? Si tu avais été là, je n'aurais pas eu à expliquer ce que j'ai vu de la façon dont je l'ai vu ; tu l'aurais vu aussi.

Language in the Meanwhile (16)

Why do we put effort into making things correspond with people with whom we do not correspond? If you had been there, I would not have had to explain what I saw in the way that I saw it; you would have seen it too.

I walked. Past more museums and universities, McDonalds and Burger Kings, bookstores and boulangeries. Finally I reached the Boulevard Edgar Quinet, the street on the edge of the Montparnasse Cemetery, and turned quietly inside. I had Googled the location of Julio Cortázar's grave that morning and found it listed on a website called findagrave.com: 6447, Section 2E. I spent a moment conferring with the map, measuring the distance between Cortázar and the star that told me I was here. I said a quiet *bonjour* to the old groundskeeper with his green watering can, then walked silently through the rows of raised-up tombs.

    I wanted to see Cortázar buried next to Carol Dunlop. Cortázar had been much older than Dunlop when they met and fell instantly in love. He'd written her a letter asking her to leave her family and the life that she had always known to go and be with him. He said he knew it sounded like a dream but that sometimes, with just a little push, a dream can transform into reality.

Cortázar: I love him, but he frustrates the hell out of me sometimes. In *Hopscotch*, I identify most with the unseen figure of Morelli, who appears on the margins, in the shadows, as a stand-in for Cortázar. He comments on the process of building a novel out of fragments. At some point, he simply disappears from the scene.

I guess I wanted Cortázar to be more up-front about his novel-writing desires, rather than masking them in the figure of Morelli. I wanted to hear him describe his process in first-person. It's hard not to be annoyed with him too when he spouts this patriarchal crap about how women are no good at reading. Through the voice of Morelli, he says female readers are passive while male readers are the ideal critical ones. It pisses me off that the person who wrote this also convinced an intelligent woman to marry him by writing her a letter, as if he depended on the woman's passive acceptance in order to succeed.

Fuck you, Cortázar, I mumbled as I kicked the edge of his grave. What if Dunlop had written the letter to you, instead of you writing to her? Would you have gone to her, the same way she gave up everything to come to you? Would you have been brave enough to pick up your life and redistribute it in the unfamiliar light of an elsewhere?

Before Alex took off on his flight home to Florence, he sent me a message containing no words, only a series of images: the Ted Berrigan tattoo on his arm, mailing the letter; his copy of Pavese's *Disaffections*; an airport sign that read IF YOU SEE SOMETHING, SAY SOMETHING; and the right half of his face beside the window in his seat on the plane.

There was a café called Le Tournesol outside the Montparnasse Cemetery, on Rue de la Gaité. I settled into a table on the patio to eat and smoke and think about what I'd seen; what I'd done. When I spoke to the waiter in French, he asked if I was Italian.

You look Italian, he said. You're not Italian?

Alex would have gotten a kick out of that, if I messaged him about it, which I wouldn't.

Non, I replied, *je suis américaine*.

Americana, he sang, Americana, his voice floating up and down as he walked toward the kitchen in the back to put in my order.

Me, he said when he returned to the patio where I was sitting alone. I'm Italian, he said, as if I didn't know. I'm from Sicily. Where are you from? he asked me.

Chicago, I replied.

Chicago, Chicago! You know, I am related to Al Capone. He thumped his chest.

The waiter lingered at the table while I lit a cigarette and looked out at the street. Police were blocking off the avenue, getting ready for a protest.

You in America, he said, you are hating Trump. We in France, we are hating Macron.

He leaned in the doorway and watched the protestors gathering while I ate a tartine and read a chapbook by Anne Carson about Proust's character Albertine. The waiter began to sing a song in Italian to which he'd added my name.

It's not good to read while eating, he said, and I set down my book.

It's not good for the brain and the stomach to multi-task, he said. To digest at the same time. He tapped his head and his stomach in succession.

I couldn't sleep that night, so I wrote a letter to Alex in my head while staring at the slanted ceiling in Isabelle's loft.

Dear Alex, I thought, I tried to read your old messages today, but the messaging app on my phone would not cooperate with me. I tried to read them online, but the website was down for required maintenance.

I don't really know how to explain to you the way it feels when I not only think I shouldn't contact you but I am also unable to privately access your messages from an earlier time. I don't know how to explain this to you, but I'll try.

It's like all those scenes in movies when someone runs alongside a quickening train to keep up with the person inside who is mouthing unheard words behind the window. It's like Jesse says to Celine in *Before Sunset*, describing her appearance in his dream: "You go by, and you go by, and you go by…"

This scene happens in two ways. One involves the person inside the train finally saying the one thing they've been wanting to say for so long, but the person running alongside the train cannot hear it. They keep running and shouting, What? What are you saying? What are you saying?! I can't hear you! and gesturing frantically toward their ear. Meanwhile, the person inside the train keeps saying the unheard words over and over. The viewer of the film—completely removed from the situation—is the only one who has any idea of what's going on. The train picks up speed, hurtling faster than the person's legs can run, so the person stops running and stands, panting, on the platform. The train disappears, and the person on the platform is left to fill in all those gaps of silence.

In the other version of this scene, the person inside the train says nothing at all. They press one hand against the glass. They speak with their eyes—a language only the two people who live inside it can decipher. Then the person inside the train peels their palm away from the window and steps away. The train speeds out of sight—gone.

Langue entre-temps (17)

Regarde le monde : regarde ses matins, ses mimosas, son ciel gris. Prends cette journée d'été orageuse et il s'avère que je tombe. J'essaie d'être introspective, auto-interrogative. J'ai incarné tellement de personnes différentes tout ce temps. Voilà, une nouvelle photo d'auteur : un écrivain très sérieux, ne portant pas de noir. Une trop grande abstraction.

Language in the Meanwhile (17)

Look at the world: look at its mornings, mimosas, gray skies. Take this stormy summer day and it turns out I'm falling. I try to be introspective, self-interrogating. I've been so many different people all this time. Here, a new author photo: a very serious writer not wearing black. Too great an abstraction.

Before I left Isaac in the Hudson Valley, I'd been thinking about doing so for some time. He knew; we'd spoken about it many times. He wasn't happy either, and all we wanted after our own happiness was for the other person to be happy too. When things were tense between us at home, I would go to my friend Amy's house nearby to talk and drink wine, play with her dogs, and sort out our feelings. On one of those nights, we calculated our astro-cartography charts. One step beyond mere astrology, the charts would tell us—based on the arrangement of planets at the time of our birth—the global locations where we would be most likely to find love and career success; the places where we could shed our origins and start anew; and the places it would be best if we avoided. Colorful lines representing Mercury, Venus, Saturn, and other planets I know nothing about intersected across maps of Europe, North and South America, and the Middle East. My chart told me that, without a doubt, Chicago was one of the best and most pleasant places to stay in terms of the global horoscope. In Chicago, I would certainly spend a happy and relaxing time. I would be surrounded by an aura of confidence, freedom, and loyalty.

My Venus line, on the other hand—the one representing love, pleasure, and romance—didn't navigate any paths through the United States or any other continent. Instead, it leapt off the tip of Alaska, straight down into the ocean, touching no other land mass along its way.

Maybe the love of your life is living in Alaska, Amy said.

Maybe I'm supposed to go on a cruise that leaves from Alaska? I replied.

A writing residency cruise that leaves from Alaska! Amy declared.

Great, I said. Stay tuned for my forthcoming memoir: My Self-Destructive Venus Line: a Love Story on the North Pacific.

But I didn't want to write a memoir. I wanted someday to write a novel because people are like novels: you never know which parts are real and which are fake. You just pick the parts you like, and go on believing.

My mother helped me with the move to Chicago. I couldn't afford movers, and she liked the work; she always had, despite her claims otherwise. Each time we moved my furniture into a new, empty space—grumpy and sweaty and shouting at each other, always in the summer—she would say, You know you have to live here for the rest of your life; I'm not doing this again.

I will, I'd say, I promise. But I knew it wasn't true.

The weekend I left, Isaac and I agreed that he would stay with a friend to give me the space for all the boxes. It took three hours just to pack up all the books while my mother worked on the kitchen, asking me every three minutes if a certain spoon or appliance belonged to me or to Isaac. For what seemed like a long time, the only words I spoke aloud were his, mine, mine, his, mine. But then I started telling her about graduate school; about the classes I hoped I would take; the authors I would get to work with and meet in the city; the countries I hoped to travel to for translation projects; the states where I might get a job one day; the friends I'd been meaning to visit all over the U.S., how maybe now I'd have the time to see them. She turned from the red blender she was packing and smiled, but her eyes were soft and the smile was sad.

Honey, she said, one of these days you'll decide to stop running.

Alex had a mission, the year he lived in Chicago, on top of all his coursework and his translation project on Pavese. He wanted to cull together an anthology of contemporary American poetry, translating each poem himself from English to Italian, on facing pages, and writing an introduction on the current trends in urban American poetry. He already had a small publisher in Florence that was interested in the idea—a press that was run by a friend of a friend or something. They wanted Alex to send a few poems now and again, to show that he was working on the project, and to provide a few thoughts about what shape the book might take.

I would go with Alex to readings in Chicago, two or three times a week, to scout for poets he might want to include in the anthology. We looked intimidating, I would think to myself at these readings, standing in a corner dressed all in black. Alex only ever wore black jeans, black boots, and long- or short-sleeve black button-down shirts, depending on the season. He said he needed the space in his brain that is often taken up by clothing choices to be free and open for poetry. We drank PBR tallboys with discerning looks on our faces. If the reading was bad, Alex would insist we leave early. We would detour to the nearest bar where I would drink another tallboy and listen to Alex rant about his frustrations with what he called lazy poetry. He thought a lot of poets were lazy, employing easy images and performatively ironic or nihilistic phrases they knew would go over well in a crowd. He wasn't wrong.

But if the reading was good, Alex would want to stay for a long time afterwards to talk to the poets and ask if they would contribute to his anthology. Some were turned off by Alex's intensity, but the right people would be drawn to him. I would often talk with Alex and the poets after the reading, smoothing out any miscommunications that would inevitably arise when Alex became too excited to finish one sentence before beginning a new one. Other times, the conversation would hurtle beyond my energy level, and I would step outside to slow things down by smoking a cigarette and letting the smoke filter into the breeze. I would wait for Alex to finish his conversation, toss a few wrinkled dollar bills down on the bar, and join me outside for another cigarette before heading out in the same direction to our separate homes.

Dear Alex: I brought our poetry professor's *book of failures* with me to France. I've been rereading it and thinking of you. You told me once you were obsessed with failure, and I am too: I'm obsessed with opening myself up to all the possibilities that emerge from failure. My friends often tell me that I'm brave because of this. I don't know.

All I know is that this life is full of endless revisions; recalculations.

That professor used to remind us—remember?—that we had to love something else as much as we loved writing; that writing should never be the only thing we love. This is hard for me, but I'm trying: I love dancing to a song that gets me completely out of my head. I love the moment I know that the meal I am cooking is ready. I love steeping a pot of loose leaf tea and carrying it out to a good friend who came to see me. I love light roast coffee beans and the blues of summer evenings. I love the snow. I love holding a friend in my arms when they're about to leave, or when they've just returned from a long time away. I love when someone makes me laugh so hard that I cry and my stomach clenches in pain. I love to fall asleep in freshly-laundered sheets. I love rain. I love thunderstorms. I love rain.

In the *book of failures*, she says that nothing written will bring love. She says that love comes when you abandon the delusion, when you realize that you can proceed, even creatively, without it. I used to think about this on the train after you left, on my way home from meeting with her. I think better on the El. My thoughts are clearer; sharper; more precise. I would peer out the window at the porches and back doors and landings of this city that I love for reasons I never seem to be able to explain. My life in Chicago is a story I keep trying and failing to tell because I don't know how to tell stories. I've never been good at developing narratives. I always tell everything out of order, in the wrong way. When you lived in Chicago, you laughed at me for this.

You know, you would say to me, the reason people tell stories, and the reason people like them, is because of their details.

Important details; factual details; descriptive and engaging, crucial details—that's what I am always leaving out. But I think I'm on my way, I think I am *en train de*, I think I am *en train de comprendre*, I think I'm on my way to understanding.

Langue entre-temps (18)

Il y a des années, tu m'as envoyé le passage d'*Anna Karénine* sur la difficulté de parler sincèrement et honnêtement ; le terrible constat que nous sommes souvent obligés de dire le contraire de ce que nous pensons. J'ai porté ce passage avec moi, insaisissable, depuis longtemps. Mais je pense aussi à cette conversation dans le livre qui se déroule sans paroles du tout, seulement des mots abrégés en lettres gribouillées à la craie, puis effacées. Les symboles à la craie, associés à la compréhension des yeux, épellent la première lettre des mots qu'ils veulent dire ; rien de superflu ou de mal compris. J'aimerais pouvoir toujours parler ainsi.

Language in the Meanwhile (18)

Years ago, you sent me the passage from *Anna Karenina* about the difficulty of speaking truly and honestly; the terrible fact that we are often forced to say the opposite of what we mean. I have carried this passage with me, intangibly, for a long time. But I also think about the conversation in this book that takes place without speech at all, only words abbreviated into letters scrawled in chalk then washed away. The chalk symbols, paired with understanding in the eyes, spell the first letter of the words they wish to say; nothing superfluous or misunderstood. I wish that I could always speak this way.

Isabelle wanted to bring me to the Musée Jacquesmart-André to catch a special exhibition on Hammershøi—the Danish painter of solitude, silence, and light.

Hammershøi's paintings, which he completed one at a time and very slowly, all in soft and muted colors, depict largely empty spaces: interiors with large windows; bare furniture in slightly odd, slightly un-liveable arrangements; the backs of women as they think about doing something else, later, out of frame.

But I'll correct myself: he didn't paint many women, but rather one woman—Ida, his wife; presumably because she was there, like a chair. I shouldn't presume to know anything about their relationship or the dynamic between them when he painted her. But I love the way that light in his paintings floods an empty room; the way Ida looks off to the side, or straight ahead, or into a corner.

Isabelle and I had talked about Hammershøi's paintings before, but she wanted to see them in person with me in Paris because she'd written about them in her book. In fact, the cover art was a rendition of one of our favorites: *Interior with Young Woman Seen from the Back*. We were hoping to use the same artwork for the English translation. We walked through all six rooms, spending time with *Ida Reading a Letter*, with *Moonlight, Strandgade 30*, and *Interior from Strandgade with Sunlight on the Floor*. In front of the *Interior with Young Man Reading*, Isabelle said she might write a follow-up to *Language in the Meanwhile* in the voice of Alex, and that she would ideally want the *Young Man Reading* for the cover.

We sat down on a cushioned bench to gaze at the *Tall Windows*, and Isabelle told me her thoughts on Hammershøi. For other painters, she said, when a woman is seen by an open window, it is to show a spiritual or romantic longing; a yearning. But this is not the way it is with Hammershøi, and I like that. When he places Ida by a window, it is to help him draw a contrast between the bright sun of the day outside and the soft, gray shades of the interior. Do you see? The woman is a focal point for the artist. But for the viewer, she is an arrangement of light and shadow in the room.

Isabelle went on to say these paintings had inspired much of her book: now that I was seeing them in person for the first time, I would be able to create a more truthful and accurate translation. Over dinner, I showed her a small fragment I'd completed at home after the museum:

> J'aime grimper à l'intérieur des tableaux et taquiner l'image pour la séparer de sa forme. À l'intérieur d'un tableau, je deviens plus.

> I like to climb inside paintings and tease apart the image from its form. Inside a painting, I become more.

Très bien, she said with a slow smile. We're becoming more. *Nous devenons plus.*

Are you listening, Alex? I watched a strange film the other night called *Certified Copy*. It was similar to the films in Linklater's *Before* trilogy, but this one did not believe as much in love and possibility. In *Certified Copy*, a couple of anxious, disillusioned, middle-aged people spend the day together in a small Italian town—a classic cinematic storyline in which the two characters "unexpectedly" fall in love by the end. But this film doesn't make it so easy. It emphasizes all the tensions that arise from their fears and anxieties.

Their ending is uncertain.

There's a turning point in a café when they're mistaken for a long-married couple. Instead of laughing it off or playing along with amusement, they play along with sadness and anger. They pit their anger against one another, taking out their hurts and fears on each other. They stop speaking as strangers and start speaking as that fictional, long-married couple. What's strange is how believable that fictional reality becomes: I believe them immediately. Then again, it's not difficult for me to believe in fiction when the fiction is rooted in reality.

Maybe what struck me was how easy it became for them to say what they wanted to say once that fictional frame had been introduced. Before, when they were strangers, they had such difficulty speaking to each other. But once they were no longer quite themselves (and, at the same time, the most themselves they'd ever been), words came easily.

So which version is more true? Both are real to me: strangers stammering over their words, performing identities; and people who know each other intimately, speaking clearly about difficult things. I think this is why I love translation. I circle and stammer too much in my own language, but when I speak French, I become the strong and clear voice I am trying to be.

The night after the museum, back home at the apartment, Isabelle and I had another glass of wine while she gave me a Tarot reading. I shuffled the cards while thinking of my question, which was something like, Will things work out with my writing? or, Will things work out with my writing and love life? or, Do I even want a love life, or do I just want to write? I spread the cards out in a long line on the coffee table, pulled out two as she instructed, and placed them in the designated positions until she told me it was time to turn them face up. The first card I turned over was The Tower: your current life is crumbling beneath you; time for transformation. The second card was The Lovers in reverse: you're at a crossroads in love; time to make a decision.

I told Isabelle about the PhD from German Studies who I'd slept with a couple of times after Alex left the city.

He was not a good fuck, I told her, and she laughed.

The first night, he puked up his Thai food in the kitchen

sink immediately afterwards, like fucking for seven minutes had been too much for him. I was so shocked that I just laid there while he brushed his teeth and washed his hands and face, then climbed back into bed to put his arm around me. He said he hoped it would be a funny story we might share one day.

Mais non ! Isabelle shouted in laughter, he did not!

Mais oui ! I said, *C'est vrai !* But I gave him the benefit of the doubt and slept with him a second time.

Non non non, Isabelle continued laughing. You did not!

Listen, I said, finally laughing myself, I thought, perhaps, that some people get better at fucking with practice and time.

I am guessing he did not, Isabelle said as she smiled and sipped her wine.

I shook my head.

Seven minutes—again! I told her. He kept saying my name over and over, like thirty times, droning it like he was saying the Mass in Latin. And he couldn't stimulate me at all. I'm serious. He so successfully avoided stimulating my clitoris that I don't think he even knew it existed.

Isabelle could not contain her laughter.

It gets better, there's one more thing, I said.

Non ! she said. There couldn't be.

Just this, I said, putting on a performative air for the the punch line. He lay beside me afterwards, moaning breathlessly, and said, "That was incredible."

Isabelle covered her eyes and shook her head.

You have to wonder, I said, leaning back into the couch, done with my story, how two people could experience the same event so differently.

Oui, she said, *c'est nul*.

Anyway, I said, I didn't sleep with anyone for a while after that.

For some reason, I didn't tell Isabelle the real end of that story, which was this: the next day, I received the only piece of mail that Alex ever sent me, all the way from Florence. It was an Italian copy of Barthes' *A Lover's Discourse*, with a brief note—a quote from Pavese:

> Even something harsh and difficult is a comfort if we choose it ourselves. If it is imposed on us by others, it is agony.

Alex, what am I doing writing all these letters to you in my head? I must have thought-scrawled at least three to you today alone, maybe more.

Viktor Shklovsky wrote a book of letters to Elsa Triolet but changed her name, like I've changed yours, to Alya. This Elsa, or rather Alya, forbid him to speak of his love for her, so he wrote to her every day of anything else—literature; politics; philosophy; the rain. But underlying every subject was the one he truly wanted to express.

You never told me not to speak about *mon amour pour toi*. Still, it never seemed as though it was something I should do. In my research I discovered that every book of letters seems to require some kind of constraint. Maybe my constraint is that my letters to you will only ever be thought and never written. Because they will never be written, and therefore never sent nor received, perhaps you will believe I am no longer thinking of you; that perhaps I never do.

But Alex: the opposite is true. I am thinking of you even when I do not realize I am thinking of you. It would be easy to look at my life and define it by what it lacks. But the truth is that I choose to fill my life with empty spaces because they allow me to write to you.

In Shklovsky's book, a confusion develops between his real self and his written one. "I see myself at a remove; I fear my destiny. I fear its literary quality." He writes that he is becoming part of a book. There is a comfort in becoming this for me. There is a kind of relief, like sinking into a warm bath at the end of the day. I shed the everyday. I become the version of myself that can't be spoken; the version that is only known by you.

My brain was steeped in French the year that Alex lived in Chicago, but I made a little room for learning about the history of Italian. One night in the spring, we sat in the square eating scoops of gelato from the shop beside the fountain, and Alex told me the reason why the Italian language had developed in such an unconventional fashion.

You think of Italy as one cohesive country, yes? he said, drawing the shape of a boot in the air with his spoon. Of course it is one cohesive country now, he said, but until about 1850 or something like that, Italy was divided into all these multiple, different kingdoms. And each kingdom had its own version of Italian; its own way of speaking. And these languages were so different from each other that you could not understand the ones you did not speak. In fact, my mother and my father are from two different regions in Italy, and even today, many generations later, they will sometimes use a word or phrase or pronunciation from their region when they are speaking to each other, and the confusion that ensues between them is crazy—one will shout at the other that they don't know what they're saying, they don't know what they mean, while the other will shout back that it's because they speak an inferior tongue.

He tossed his empty cup and spoon in the nearby garbage. So there was no official, cohesive government language over the whole land, he said, only the many languages from these regions. Each was developed based on the different ways that people wished to express themselves. And the people who expressed themselves most publicly were the poets and writers. So the poets and writers are the ones we have to thank for shaping a style and vocabulary based on beauty, and sound, and rich imagery, and this is why Italian to this day is a language full of poetry.

For example, he said, this is the best example. In the early 1800s, when Alessandro Manzoni was almost done writing *I promessi sposi*—in English it is called *The Betrothed* or something, it is the first Italian novel—he said he had to go to Florence to wash the book's language in the river Arno.

So that's what you're referring to, I said, tossing my own cup and spoon into the garbage, when you say you need to wash your language in the river.

Think about it, Alex said. For you especially, so much of your writing is about rivers and bridges. Imagine a clothesline stretching from your window to a bridge over a river. You dip your writing, all those pages, in the water and you swirl them around, you wash them, till they're ready. Then you hang them on the line.

Alex and I were walking down Giddings now—a loop we often took when we knew it was nearly time to go home but hadn't finished our conversation yet. We paused in front of my favorite window with the plant-filled alcove and the paper lantern that cast a dreamy, orange glow. Alex lit a cigarette, handed it to me, then lit another for himself. He gestured toward the window with his smoking hand, the ember almost blending with the window's glow.

How do the poems dry? he said.

Langue entre-temps (19)

Que se passerait-il si nous nous revoyions ? Serait-on silencieux, ne sachant quoi dire ? Aurions-nous l'impression de nous connaître ? Ou serions-nous gênés, mal à l'aise, voire effrayés, de la même façon que l'on croise l'ombre d'un étranger qui se rapproche dans une rue obscure de la ville ?

Language in the Meanwhile (19)

What would happen if we saw each other again? Would we be silent, not knowing what to say? Would we feel as though we know each other? Or would we feel awkward, uncomfortable, even afraid—the same way one encounters the shadow of a stranger moving closer on a dark city street?

When I arrived in Paris, because I was in Europe, I thought I must be closer to Alex than I had been for quite some time. A nonstop flight from Paris to Florence cost less than 100 euros and would take less than two hours. But a train from Paris to Florence would be eight or nine hours—the same amount of time it had taken me to fly to Paris from the U.S. Google Maps told me I could catch a train from Gare de Lyon and cross the border into Italy in only five hours and forty-three minutes—only six stops on the train. At Torino Porta Susa I would change to an Italian train, present my passport, and in two hours and fifty minutes (only five stops on that train), I would arrive at Firenze Santa Maria Novella station. From there I could exit the station, cross the river Arno that divides the city in two, and arrive in the Metropolitan City of Florence.

I imagined Alex meeting me there, beside the river Arno. I imagined us walking and talking together the way we had before. I imagined that nothing would have changed between us; that he would be happy to see me and to show me his city the way that I had shown him mine. I imagined the bells of Santa Maria Novella tolling the evening hour I arrived, as if heralding some important message or occasion. I even imagined arriving in Florence without telling Alex I was on my way, like in my dream. I imagined we would run into each other by the river, or rounding the corner of some curved, cobblestone street. I saw the scene as if from the outside, from above; as if it were a movie. The soundtrack would be Sufjan Stevens, obviously.

I looked up Airbnbs that would match the aesthetic of the film I was composing in my head and found a "magical one-guest retreat [...] an inspiring artist studio" where I could "wake up to the surreal view of the entire Duomo and Cathedral." The Airbnb was in a building from the 1600s on Piazzo Duomo ("the true heart of the historical center—Leonardo da Vinci lived only two houses down!!") with large, double-paned windows overlooking the populated piazza below. The host promised that if I kept the windows open, I would hear church bells, violinists, and accordions in the crowd that would linger past midnight. The listing included many images of solitary women posing in the windows with their long hair tumbling down their backs, their faces tilted upwards toward the view. Maybe Alex and I would meet in the morning on the Ponte Vecchio, or the Ponte alle Grazie, and then what would we do? That was where my imagination always stopped, unable to conjure a believable story.

I feel tempted, in my dreams, to become a Subject; to become a figure that is separate from my Self. I would be like a silhouette, an arrangement of light and shadow, inside a picture frame hanging on the wall.

What would we do together in Florence, the figure of Alex and the figure of me? I couldn't come up with an answer because in order to be in Florence with Alex, he would have had to have chosen me.

That's clunky. Let me try it in French: *il aurait dû me choisir*. Much cleaner—streamlined, simplified. I like the way that French is sometimes wordier than English, but this phrase—*il aurait dû me choisir*—smoothes out my inability to process the idea in my first language. *Il aurait dû me choisir*, but he did not, *mais il n'avait pas*, and he would not, *et il ne voulait pas*. But I wondered how to express this idea in Italian.

French and Italian might both be Romance languages, but there are enough differences that if a French speaker and an Italian speaker tried to hold a conversation with each other in their own separate languages, they would not, under most circumstances, understand each other. So I put the sentence "He would have had to have chosen me," with all its uncertain qualities of hesitation, into my preferred online translation website and came up with three possibilities: 1) *avrebbe dovuto scegliere me* (he should have chosen me), 2) *mi avrebbe dovuto scegliere* (he would have to choose me), 3) *avrebbe dovuto scegliermi* ([he] should have chosen me). Each possibility was so direct; so clear and confident, unafraid of what outcome might befall the speaker. I thought about Alex's intensity—how difficult some found him, because Americans pretend they are humble when all we really care about is ourselves. Alex never pretended; his speech was clear and candid. My American friends didn't know him well at all, but some said they thought he was too much. Now that I'd explored a little Italian, I knew they were wrong. He wasn't full of ego; he was full of clarity, and he should have chosen me.

On the flight to Paris, I reread a John Ciardi article I'd saved from my translation class, again marking the passage about the gulf between English and Italian: "We tend to consider," Ciardi said, "only the top slice of a given word." Slice. Alex hated the English word 'slice.'

> Poets, on the other hand, are likely to use words in depth: they are interested in the images locked inside a word, in its muscularity, in its history, in its connotations, and in its levels of usage. As soon as one begins to hunt the American-English language for words that are equivalent *in depth* to Italian words, he learns that whatever he does manage to get across the language boundary will not be got across by any simple one-for-one transliteration.

In Chicago, I'd often taken Alex to a place I loved but did not want to explain to anyone in English; the square; the window on Giddings Avenue; the bridge over the river on Wilson, where the train descended from the elevated tracks down to the street; Montrose Harbor, with its rocks and its pier leading out to the lighthouse. In these places, by observing the way that Alex took them in, I knew he understood them in the same way I did. At least it felt that way to me. If it was not the same way exactly, it was still a way that prioritized silence over speaking—which, in these locations, I felt was the most important thing.

I'd brought others to my favorite places before, and it had always been enormously disappointing. They would open their mouths to speak and something totally off-topic would tumble out, as if we were standing not in a place that was sacred to me but in some bar or walking through some alley. You ever partied here? one of them asked me once, and it depressed me so much that I spent the rest of the day in bed with the lights low, listening to Yo La Tengo.

Isabelle and I sat by the Canal one early evening, examining a few pages of my translation and discussing the different theories we'd studied in school.

She asked me how I dealt with the gray areas of translation; how no decision could ever be deemed completely accurate. I showed her another passage from the Ciardi article and watched her read, her brown eyes gazing intently at the page while the rest of her body seemed to keep moving in small, almost imperceptible ways: one foot bumping up against the bench; three fingers quietly tapping the page; her hair moving back and forth with the wind or a tiny movement of her shoulders. The Ciardi passage said:

I had no theory at that point—only a feeling. And I still have no theory I can securely defend. The rest was trial and error, something like learning to walk a tightrope if one can only manage to grab the rope when he falls, and if he can then manage to get up, and if he falls only forward, there is always the possibility that he will make it to the other side.

I rarely felt like I was falling, in an unproductive way, in France, and this surprised me, but it also made me glad. I understood the signs on all the shop doors and street corners. I knew how to ask for what I wanted, and I did so clearly, with the other person always seeming to understand me. It occurred to me that if I went to Italy, I wouldn't understand the signs that I was seeing, and that even if I walked around the city of Florence with someone I knew—with someone who knew me—I couldn't guarantee that I wouldn't fall backward instead of forward.

Isabelle looked up at me after reading the passage from Ciardi.

It is good you are here, she said quietly.

Even if I have no theory I can securely defend? I asked, picking up the last bite of cheese. Even then, she said, popping the last fresh fig into her mouth and standing up to begin packing our things.

On y va, she said, let's get a baguette *pour le matin* before all the boulangeries in the neighborhood are closed, and we walked down the street, her arm in mine.

Walking home from the boulangerie, Isabelle tore off the rounded edge of the baguette and handed it to me. It was still warm.

I used to walk with Alex for hours around this part of the city when he was here, she said, lighting a cigarette and looking around as if he might appear in the crowd or step out of a shop and into our path. He said Americans were wrong to say Parisians seem glum and unhappy—that they seemed so much happier than New Yorkers. He said he thought they had a better sense of, how would you say, priorities. He didn't really seem to want to go home. But it's practically impossible for foreigners to get an apartment here—all the landlords take a lifetime to get you the keys. And he had to finish his degree back home, I know. Besides, I think he had a relative that was sick or something. Still, when we would walk around the city at night or during the day, talking at length or falling into a comfortable silence, I could not help thinking that this is the life I want to live every day. When you are young and in love with chasing an idea, every day feels like a holiday; far from the everyday concerns of other people. I wanted to be on holiday with Alex for the rest of my life, whatever that means, but I was hanging on for dear life to the rope and he was falling forward faster, without me.

Langue entre-temps (20)

Souviens-toi que « tout ce qui vaut la peine d'être fait vaut la peine d'être mal fait. » (Jack Gilbert). Souviens-toi que « Wordsworth s'est épuisé à chercher toute la journée pour trouver une comparaison au rossignol. » (encore Gilbert). Nous attendons que les bons mots viennent, mais ils ne viennent pas toujours, et pourtant, nous nous épuisons à les attendre. Parfois, attendre et essayer nous fatigue tout autant, quand nous travaillons trop dur dans la mauvaise direction. J'ai travaillé si dur dans la mauvaise direction. « Est-ce la lucidité, la simplicité, l'achèvement ou l'incompréhension ? » (encore Gilbert). Bonne question, et je crois que c'est l'incompréhension. Plutôt que la lucidité, je préfère la recherche de la vérité - une enquête sur des questions sans réponse. « C'est à cause de mon cœur imparfait qui préfère cette distance des gens. Qui préfère les demi-réunions qui ne peuvent mener à l'intimité. Amitiés provisoires interrompues dès le début. Un plaisir de ne pas communiquer. » (toujours Gilbert).

Language in the Meanwhile (20)

Remember that "anything worth doing is worth doing badly." (Jack Gilbert). Remember that "Wordsworth wore himself out searching all day to find a simile for nightingale." (Gilbert again). We wait for the right words to come, but they do not always come and still, we tire ourselves out with the waiting. Sometimes waiting and trying tire us equally, when we are working too hard in the wrong directions. I have worked so hard in the wrong directions. "Is the clarity, the simplicity, an arriving or an emptying out?" (Gilbert again). A good question, and I do believe it is an emptying. Instead of clarity, I prefer the search for Truth—an investigation into unanswered questions. "Blame it on my imperfect heart which prefers this distance from people. Prefers the half-meetings which cannot lead to intimacy. Provisional friendships interrupted near the beginning. A pleasure in not communicating." (always Gilbert).

The morning I was set to leave for the residency, Isabelle accompanied me to the Gare de l'Est. We were early; the gate number for my train toward Bellefort-Ville was not yet showing up on the screen, so we had an espresso while we waited to find out where I needed to go.

I thanked Isabelle for letting me stay.

I don't really know how to say what all this has meant to me, I told her.

She squeezed my hand.

For me too, she said. I don't want you to go, but you have work to do.

Yes, I agreed.

And you will tell me everything, she said, and we will see each other again, here or there, we will see each other somewhere.

She squeezed my hand again.

I blinked, and the number 10 appeared on the screen next to Bellefort-Ville.

Isabelle dragged my suitcase behind her as she walked me to my gate.

Ma chérie, she said, write me when you get there.

I will, I said, and we kissed each other on the cheeks and held each other tightly, as we had when I first arrived in Paris. But I was not going home; I was moving further forward on my tightrope, so it did not feel precisely like goodbye.

Another passenger helped me stow my suitcase on the rack and I settled into a seat by the window. I folded down the tray table in front of me and pulled out the book I planned to read. The train intercom sounded three ascending tones. I felt the train begin to move beneath me and pressed my left hand against the window. Isabelle was still standing on the platform. Her mouth moved, but I couldn't tell what she was saying. I peeled my palm away from the glass as the train picked up speed and Paris disappeared behind me.

It was during one of the bad poetry nights, afterwards at the bar, that I asked Alex when he was planning to solicit a poem from me. I was nearly done drinking my second tallboy.

I mean, you don't honestly plan to create an anthology of contemporary American poetry without including a poem from me, I said facetiously. He smirked, but that night, it annoyed me.

Oh I don't know, he teased me, only the best can be included. If you have something you would like me to consider, you can send it my way, but I'm afraid there can be no guarantees.

I punched him in the arm and he laughed, but before we could speak about it further, an already-drunk bachelorette party barreled into the bar. A red-haired girl in heels, wearing several strings of beads around her neck, lurched into our table, toppling Alex's can and spilling its contents. After a hasty attempt on her part to help us clean, we succeeded in convincing her to return to her own party and their celebratory drinking, and we got out of there, quickly, without speaking.

I woke the next morning to an email Alex had sent me at 4:16. The subject line read: "for the anthology."

I want you to write something new for me, he wrote. It has to be your best. Maybe it will be today. Maybe it will be tomorrow. Maybe it will happen several weeks or months from today. You will know it when you see it. You know what I mean. When you find my poem, send it to me. Before you write it down, I want you to show me. No matter where I am, no matter where you are, no matter what hour of the day or night, I want for you to send the poem to me.

Langue entre-temps (21)

Je parcours les poèmes de Jack Gilbert pour dire ce que je veux dire – une manœuvre sinueuse, sachant que tu possèdes le même exemplaire de son recueil de poèmes, t'imaginant chercher les poèmes auxquels je fais référence ici et les lire avec moi. C'est la meilleure façon de comprendre les choses. Alors j'appelle l'arbre un noyer cendré, ce que je ne pense pas qu'il soit, en attendant d'avoir moins peur de t'envoyer ces lettres. Je photographie le sapin et je te l'envoie. À la façon de Keats, je laisse des espaces vides dans mes journées pour m'accrocher à mes questions. Je me plonge dans mon travail, je passe de longues heures à mon bureau, sachant à quel point la vie réelle est sinueuse.

Mais cette lettre est également sinueuse. J'aimerais te parler, et il y a tant de choses que je n'ai pas dites dans ces pages.

J'ai essayé de trouver une langue entre-temps qui soit audible.

Language in the Meanwhile (21)

I'm working my way through Jack Gilbert's poems as a way of saying what I want to say—a sideways maneuver, knowing you own the same copy of his collected poems as I do, imagining you seeking out the poems I am referencing here and reading with me. It's the best way I know how to make sense of things. So I call the tree a butternut, which I don't think it is, waiting to feel less afraid to send you these letters. I photograph the fir tree and send it on to you. Like Keats, I leave blank spaces in my days to hold on to my questions. I delve into my Work, put in long hours at my desk, knowing how much of Actual Life is sideways.

But this letter is sideways too. I'd like to talk with you, and there is so much I haven't said in these pages.

I tried for language in the meanwhile that can be heard.

On the train from Paris to the residency a few hours away, I reread a favorite novel by an author I admire. The novel was a long internal monologue about a woman struggling to write a novel about a failed love affair. I liked the way this author moved between telling the story and reflecting on telling the story: parts she left out and why; parts she liked and didn't like to remember; all the different ways she'd tried to write and arrange material into a novel.

The copy of this novel that I own was owned by someone else before me. There are several passages highlighted in the book, first in a bright yellow and later in a faint turquoise green. I like thinking about this woman who highlighted passages in this book when it belonged to her. I felt confident it was a woman who had owned it, though there was no way for me to confirm this suspicion. I like to think about how this woman must have encountered the book when she needed it and what she must have been going through at the time, or how she may have been reflecting on something she went through at some earlier time. There was a pattern to the passages she had highlighted, first in yellow and then a faded turquoise green, which were sometimes but not always the same passages I wanted to mark during my reading. But I never highlight, only underline in black pen or draw black squares and rectangles and brackets and sometimes small stars, so that some of the highlighted passages have been left exactly as she marked them while others have been marked over, a second time, by me.

Do you think, Alex had asked me once, we pick up certain things to read in times when there would be absolutely no other thing for us to read in that moment?

I looked up at the woman in the seat across from me on the train. She was reading a novel in French and casting discerning glances at me, for what reason I do not know. I rarely understand how others see me. I looked out the window. It had been a pleasant ride. While looking out the window, I remembered it had been Alex who recommended the novel to me, a year before I found this copy at a used bookstore in downtown Chicago which I hadn't even known existed until that day. But as soon as that thought solidified in my mind, I remembered that I had, in fact, read the novel by this author I admire years before I bought it at the bookstore; that I had bought it because I was thinking about Alex again and the book reminded me of him. This meant the current reading was my fifth or sixth time with this novel. And when I remembered this, I also remembered that it was not this novel Alex had recommended to me at all but another one entirely. This changed the narrative I'd been crafting in my mind, whether for a long time or only briefly, that Alex had recommended I read a novel about a woman like me who seemed more committed to writing novels about love than she was to loving. Because Alex had not actually recommended this novel to me, the idea of his doing so became another layer of my invention of him as someone who knew me so completely I believed he would never let me go. On pages sixteen and seventeen of the novel by the writer I admire, the previous owner had highlighted the following phrases, in yellow, in this order: I'm not sure, I'm not sure, I know, I don't like remembering.

I thought a lot about what to write for Alex's anthology.

In the end, because I couldn't be sure if he'd ever read it, I sent him the poem I'd posted on Craigslist. A month later, he sent the Italian version back to me over email. I didn't hear from him for a long time after that.

CONNESSIONI PERSE: Chicago, IL: w4m; TEMI TAGLIATI FUORI

Se mi allontano abbastanza, riesco a vedere le strade che ti portano al fiume in cui ti perdi, riprendi piede in una poesia frammentata. A volte viaggio non più di 50 metri al giorno. Riempiamo i vuoti con domande, ripetiamo e rispondiamo, finché non mi ritrovo a viaggiare per le tue strade e tu riempi i miei piedi con percentuali. Se ti voltassi, potresti riprendere la strada da cui sei venuto, e potrebbe piacerti più lì la seconda volta. O forse questo è più di quanto potrei sperare. Mi sono persa, e tu sei stato nascosto dietro l'angolo a sbirciarmi. Dimmi chi stava leggendo quella notte in cui sono inciampata sulla gente del portico per salutarti, ma non l'ho fatto. Dimmi dove ero seduta a gambe incrociate sul pavimento di un soggiorno. Se mi hai vista, dimmi che ero lì.

I departed the train at Chaumont and dragged my suitcase into the lobby. I looked around for a moment until a woman in the corner spotted me and asked if I was looking for the Orquevaux residency. She waited with me while a few others joined us in the corner—all artists, mostly from the States. When all five of us were there, we piled our suitcases in two cars out on the street and began the thirty-minute drive to the château in the country.

When we arrived, a volunteer from Bulgaria showed me to my room at the top of the stairs. She stepped inside and gestured all around her at the large bed, the ornate mirrors on the wall, and the wide, wooden desk in the corner, positioned between two tall windows.

This will be your room and writing studio, she said. We only have two rooms like this.

She left me to unpack. I hung up my clothes in the adjoining dressing room and stacked my books on the desk, my notebooks in the drawer. I would be in residence at the château for six long weeks. I knew that time would move differently here; that the sun would rise at a different time and in a different way than it rose at home. Outside the window, across the valley, the steeple of an old stone church rose up from a low hill, below a mountain. I stood at the window as the church bells tolled five in the evening. Five minutes later, they tolled again.

A clear intention: that's what I was after this time around. A resonant sound, cascading over the valley. A message that would be received and understood by its recipient—whoever that recipient might turn out to be. I would produce, I promised myself, images with clarity, and my receiver would interpret the message clearly because they would see me. They would understand my utterance, and come to know me. I would transcend the muck of ambiguity, those muddy waters I'd always washed myself in; those muddy waters that often kept me from speaking coherently. I would move beyond all the distracting signifiers that kept my recipient from seeing the river in its blue-green ripples of formality. I would make the world I saw beyond the window a world that my recipient could see.

It is a matter of context, really; a willingness to include the kind of details I had always left out before. How much more; what new and different possibilities would await me, I wondered, if I faced the page with bravery, lucidity? How might my language dry and solidify if I allowed myself to wash it in these waters and hang it on the line, saying to my recipient: come here; come see; come hear the water and the bells; speak softly, and stand here next to me.

ACKNOWLEDGMENTS

The following passage referenced in this book comes from the afterword of Jenny Boully's poetry collection *of the mismatched teacups, of the single-serving spoon: a book of failures* (Coconut Books, 2012): "I know now that nothing written will bring love. Love comes when you abandon the delusion, when you realize that you can proceed, even creatively, without it."

An early version of the first poem in this book originally appeared in *Gold Wake Live*.

This book was made possible by residencies at Vermont Studio Center, Studio Faire, and Chateau Orquevaux. Warm thanks to the staff and all my fellow residents for the time, space, friendship, inspiration, and generous hospitality that supported the development of this work.

I am especially grateful to Julia Douglas and Colin Usher at Studio Faire, for their friendship and for immersing me in the lifestyle of southwest France; Ziggy Attias at Chateau Orquevaux, for insight into the legacy of Denis Diderot; Marco Palli, for insight into the history of the Italian language; Anca Untu and Vincent Illuzzi, for thoughtful and poetic edits to the passages in French and Italian; Circe Bosch, Jenny Boully, Laurence Briat, Alan Fortescue, Aviya Kushner, and Brian Teare; my friends and family; Laura Cesarco Eglin and the team at Veliz Books, for making this book a reality; and my partner, Joseph Demes, for our life in present tense.

ABOUT THE AUTHOR

Naomi Washer is the author of *TRAINSONGS* (Greying Ghost Press), *Phantoms* (dancing girl press) and *American Girl Doll* (Ursus Americanus), and the translator of Sebastián Jiménez Galindo's *Experimental Gardening Manual* (Toad Press). Her work has appeared in *Seneca Review*, *Passages North*, *Essay Daily*, *Asymptote*, and other journals. She has been awarded fellowships and residencies from Yaddo, Vermont Studio Center, Studio Faire, Chateau Orquevaux, Numeroventi, and Columbia College Chicago where she earned her MFA in Nonfiction. In 2019, she was named one of 30 Writers to Watch by The Guild Literary Complex. She lives in Chicago, where she is the editor-in-chief of *Ghost Proposal*.